"So you've hooked another big fish."

Ryan's tone was jeering as he came up beside her. "When are you going to reel him in for the kill?"

"I don't know what you're talking about," Heather said with a frown.

"I'm talking about Craven." He jerked his head to the phone in a disparaging manner. "I bet the poor fool didn't know what hit him when you turned those beautiful, scheming eyes on him."

Suddenly, Heather's temper snapped. She was tired of his accusations. "All right. So I love money," she told him flippantly. "I adore nice clothes, beautiful jewelry, a good standard of living. Why else do you think I moved in with you?" she blazed.

The words lingered in the stillness of the room.

"So, now we see the real Heather Edwards."

KATHRYN ROSS was born in Zambia, where her parents happened to live at that time, but was educated in Ireland and England, where she now lives in a village near Blackpool in Lancashire. She enjoys her work as a professional beauty therapist, but the main love of her life is writing. Kathryn doesn't remember a time when she wasn't scribbling—her first novel at the age of ten was a children's adventure story, unpublished but terrific! Traveling and the friends made through it has been a real pleasure. Candlelit dinners, log fires on a winter's night and long walks in the Lake District are also special joys. She says she's naturally romantic, enjoying reading as well as writing romantic fiction. Still single—Mr. Right hasn't come along yet—Kathryn admits her boyfriends have tough competition from her fictional heroes.

Books by Kathryn Ross

HARLEQUIN PRESENTS
1294—DESIGNED WITH LOVE

KATHRYN ROSS

no regrets

Harlequin Books

TORONTO • NEW YORK • LONDON
AMSTERDAM • PARIS • SYDNEY • HAMBURG
STOCKHOLM • ATHENS • TOKYO • MILAN

Harlequin Presents first edition October 1991
ISBN 0-373-11405-2

Original hardcover edition published in 1990
by Mills & Boon Limited

NO REGRETS

CHAPTER ONE

HEATHER glanced nervously at the clock in the lounge. It was touch and go now whether she would be on time for her appointment at Redstar. Of all the days for Susan to be late, why did it have to be today, on what could be the turning-point of her career?

She paced anxiously towards the windows and stared down at the never-ending stream of traffic heading into Manchester city centre. Her taxi was still waiting by the kerb, the meter running. She couldn't see the driver through the dark wet November morning, but she knew he would be drumming his fingertips impatiently against the steering-wheel. He had already been into her apartment twice to remind her of the cost of keeping him waiting. The price of her taxi was the least of Heather's worries; if she didn't keep this appointment with Redstar it could cost her company thousands.

She had put months of work into planning this advertising campaign for the illustrious computer company and this morning she was due at the head office to show them her ideas and hopefully sell them. If she landed this account for Craven's advertising agency it would be the largest contract they had ever handled, and the most prestigious. It would mean certain promotion for her, and God knew she did deserve it—she had worked herself ragged for it.

'Mumma.' The small voice from behind made Heather turn abruptly to glance at her daughter. 'Have I tied my shoelace right?'

Heather's heart squeezed painfully as she stared down at the adorable little face with wide blue eyes that gazed up at her appealingly. For a child who would be four in two weeks, she had made a valiant attempt at getting herself dressed. The yellow pinafore dress was buttoned up a little unevenly, and her long dark hair was tied in a pony-tail that didn't look too secure, but she had tried her best and Heather felt a lump in her throat as she moved over towards her. If only she had more time to devote to Sarah; if only things had been different.

'You've done a great job, sweetheart, but you should have waited for Susan; she will be here soon.' Please let her be here soon, she prayed silently as she corrected Sarah's buttons and bent to secure the shoelaces. She glanced at her watch and cringed. She would be fifteen minutes late for her appointment now, a thing that had never happened before. Heather Edwards prided herself on being organised and scrupulously methodical—it was one of the reasons why she had been so successful in her career while striving to bring up her daughter single-handed.

For the first time it struck her that Susan might have had an accident. The girl was a fully qualified child-minder and she had never let Heather down like this before. She was just crossing the hall to try and phone her again when the front door opened and Susan rushed in.

'I'm terribly sorry I'm late, Ms Edwards, but I'm not feeling very well this morning,' she launched in breathlessly.

One look at Susan's face made Heather forget any annoyance she might have felt. The girl did indeed look ill; her face was ashen. 'That's all right, Susan,' she said gently. 'Are you sure you're well enough to stay? You don't look too good.'

The girl nodded. 'I'll be fine now.'

'Are you sure?' Heather frowned with anxiety. She didn't look fine; she looked as if she should be in bed.

'Quite sure.' Susan smiled down at Sarah as she came to stand next to her.

'Don't worry, Mumma,' the little girl said earnestly. 'I'll look after Susan.'

The two women exchanged amused smiles. 'I couldn't be in better hands,' Susan agreed solemnly.

'In that case I'll get going,' Heather said, reaching to give her daughter a goodbye kiss.

She arrived at the Redstar buildings exactly half an hour late and her heart fluttered nervously as she walked into the impressive ground-floor reception area. There was a very real danger that Mr Adams, the chief PR executive, might refuse to see her now. In all probability his next appointment would have arrived and it could quite possibly be with a rival advertising firm. Heather knew there would be stiff competition for this contract. It would be dreadful, after all the work and preparation she had put into this project, if she were to lose her chance of trying for it through being late.

'Take a seat, Ms Edwards.' The receptionist waved to the plush settees at the far end of the room. 'I'll let Mr Adams know you're here.'

'Thank you.' Heather smiled and walked with more confidence than she felt towards the seats.

She was wearing a red cashmere dress that fell with elegant lines over her slim figure and she looked stunningly beautiful. Her jet-black hair was woven away from her oval face and into a long, thick plait revealing the exquisite bone-structure and the dark, perfectly shaped eyebrows which framed the enormous pools of her gold-flecked brown eyes. There was an almost oriental beauty about Heather; her skin was porcelain-pale and it gave her dark hair and eyes a dramatic emphasis that always drew attention. Today was no exception. Heads turned in the busy reception area as she sat quietly waiting with nervous anticipation. As always, she was unaware of the admiring glances, her mind firmly centred on her work.

Her boss wasn't going to be very pleased with her if she failed to bring in this contract. Robert Craven was a tough man to work for; there was no room in his company for anyone who was less than perfect. He was a brilliant, dynamic man and he expected everyone around him to be the same. At twenty-six, she was the youngest member of his staff to have reached such a high position. She could see everything she had worked so hard to achieve slipping away from her if she didn't get the Redstar contract.

For a moment she found herself thinking about a time four years ago when she had had nothing. No job, no home and a brand-new baby to care for. That had been one of the lowest points of her life, but she had risen above it, had carved out a successful career with determination. That time had left its mark on her though, and she would never forget it.

'Ms Edwards?' The receptionist's voice broke into her thoughts. 'I'm afraid Mr Adams won't have time to see you today. Perhaps you would like to make another appointment?'

Heather nodded, her heart sinking. Robert was going to be furious. She followed the girl back to the reception desk and waited while she consulted the appointment book.

'I'm afraid it will have to be next week now,' the girl murmured without glancing up.

Heather wrinkled her small nose disdainfully—by that time the contract would have certainly gone to someone else. 'Haven't you something sooner, even a lunchtime appointment?' she probed. 'It will be to Redstar's advantage to see my ideas before settling their account. Perhaps you should check with someone higher in authority? I'm sure the managing director would want to see me.'

The crisp confidence of Heather's voice made the other girl look up uncertainly. 'Well, I would have to check that for you, if you would like to wait a moment?'

Heather nodded, a glimmer of hope in her dark eyes. It paid to be persistent; maybe this situation would work to her advantage.

She watched as the receptionist crossed the thick red carpet, tapped at a door set discreetly back behind her desk and walked in.

From where she was standing, Heather could see a secretary busy typing at her desk. She stopped as the receptionist spoke to her and then a door opened behind them and a man walked towards them.

Heather could feel the blood draining away from her face as she watched that man, her eyes opening wide with incredulity. It couldn't be, it just couldn't! Her brain denied it frantically, yet her eyes told her quite certainly that it was indeed Ryan Jameson.

He had hardly changed at all over the last few years since she had seen him. He was still an incredibly handsome man. He had a powerful build, well over six feet with the broad shoulders of an athlete that tapered down to long, slim hips. He was not the type of man you could mistake for someone else.

Heather's stomach muscles clenched into tight knots as she stared helplessly at him, unable to move. She had loved that man so much that it had hurt—it had hurt a great deal. She should turn and walk away now before he saw her.

He lifted his head then, as if sensing someone was watching him, and his deep midnight-blue eyes locked with hers. At first they registered surprise, then they narrowed, an enigmatic expression on the ruggedly handsome face.

The receptionist was speaking to him and, although he was probably listening to her every word, his eyes never left Heather's face. They moved over its delicate oval shape, noting the hollows beneath her high cheekbones, lingering on the vulnerable curve of her soft mouth. Heather trembled. She wanted to move away, but she couldn't; her whole body was in a state of shock, immobilised by a whirlpool of emotion.

She tried desperately to analyse what she was feeling, but the emotions swirling inside her were sending confused messages to her brain. One part of her adored seeing him again, making it almost impossible to move her eyes away from him. Another part of her was terrified at this unexpected meeting, making her shiver with nerves and fear. She didn't want to see Ryan Jameson again; she didn't want to know how he was or what he was doing with his life now. She wanted to turn tail and run.

Then abruptly his eyes moved away from her and down towards his receptionist. He spoke briefly to her before turning and walking back to his office with a long, lazy stride, closing the door firmly behind him.

Heather's breath escaped in a long rush; she hadn't

realised she was holding it until this moment and she leaned weakly against the reception desk, trying to get her breathing back under normal control. She had fully expected Ryan to walk over and speak to her. That he hadn't astonished her, and she was aware of more than a tinge of disappointment which irritated her beyond words. Why should she care?

The receptionist came back towards her with an apologetic smile. 'I'm afraid Mr Jameson doesn't have any appointment free this week.'

Heather nodded and swallowed, trying to find some sort of reasonably calm voice to speak to the other woman. 'That's all right, I . . . understand,' she murmured at last. Did she understand? she wondered frantically to herself. Was Ryan making it clear that he didn't want anything to do with her? Or had he just not recognised her after all and really just had no time?

'However, if you would like to step into his office now, Mr Jameson has a few minutes to spare,' the receptionist continued.

For a moment Heather stared at the woman as if she hadn't spoken English. 'Right now, you mean?' she asked in a slightly dazed voice.

The girl nodded. 'The door is open.' She waved her hand towards the inner office, and then as the phone started to ring on her desk she turned her attention towards it, leaving Heather to walk into the next room with a heart that was pounding so hard that she felt sure the whole office block could hear it.

The private secretary in the other office got up as she walked in and with a pleasant smile knocked on her boss's door and opened it for Heather. It closed again behind her as she stepped into the bright, ultra-modern office beyond. For a moment Heather just stood inside, her dark eyes riveted to the man who sat so easily behind the large desk, his dark head resting back on the smooth cream leather chair.

'Well, well, Mrs Edwards. This is a surprise,' he drawled mockingly in that deep, velvety voice she remembered so well.

'Hello, Ryan.' Her voice was strained, her eyes dusky pools of colour in the pallor of her face. For a while she stood there, suffering the rapier blue eyes that moved very slowly up over her long legs and then intimately over the gentle curves of her body. 'Do you mind if I sit down?' Without waiting for his consent, she moved self-consciously towards the chair facing him. She seated herself, moving the portfolio that she was carrying up on to her knee, holding it across her body as if it were a shield.

'So, Heather . . .' His voice seemed to linger over her name, almost as if he were tasting it on his lips, reminding her of how he'd used to say it when they had lain close in each other's arms. 'It's been a long time.'

She nodded, unable to answer, her eyes drinking in the rugged bronze tan of his skin, the strong line of his jaw and the cleft in his firm chin that she had once traced with her lips.

'You look different.' He leaned forward and stretched out a hand, taking the portfolio from her numb fingers and placing it firmly on the desk.

'Do I?' Her voice was ragged, her breathing uneven as his eyes lingered on the full curve of her breast, almost as if he could see the delicate creamy lace of her bra and then her bare skin.

'Oh, yes.' He nodded. 'You've lost that "innocent little girl" look.'

Heather bit her lip. Of course she had changed. It was

a long time since he had last seen her—it seemed like a whole lifetime ago. Such a lot had happened to her since then. It wasn't only her body that had altered, but her whole way of thinking. She had grown up since her days with Ryan Jameson and it had been a painful process. As she looked across the wide expanse of that desk she remembered clearly the naïve girl she had once been. She remembered all the dreams that she had woven around him, girlish dreams that had flown away long ago, replaced by the harsh reality that was real life.

'I heard you got married,' he said suddenly, his eyes narrowing on the plain gold band that she had been unconsciously twisting around the third finger of her left hand. 'Who's the lucky man, then?'

'Jonathan Edwards.' She said the name with unadorned bluntness, hoping to discourage further questioning. She could see his dark brows meeting in a frown as he ran the name through his computer-like brain to see if it was anyone he should know.

'Must be quite a man.' The hard mockery was back in his voice. 'What is he, chairman of a few Swiss banks or landed gentry?'

Heather didn't like the tone of his voice or his turn of phrase and anger glinted just below her brown eyes. 'Neither, and my personal affairs are really none of your concern,' she snapped. Immediately she regretted her choice of words as she noticed the sarcastic curve of his lips, the gleam in his eyes.

'And have there been many of them over the years, Heather?' he drawled, a hard laughing edge to his voice that made her blood boil.

She controlled her temper with difficulty and ignored the question. 'My visit to Redstar isn't a social one, Ryan. I've come to discuss ideas for an advertising campaign, not to have an inane conversation. If you have no time for business, maybe you could find someone for me who has? Your superior, perhaps?' she finished in a dry tone.

'Impossible.' He leaned back in his chair, watching her with lazy indifference. It was a look she knew very well from the past. That sleepy-eyed look would make you relax and lower your guard in the mistaken belief that he wasn't really concentrating on you. When in fact he was disconcertingly attentive, taking in everything right down to the merest flicker of an eyelash.

'Nothing is impossible.' She remained perfectly calm. 'I would like to speak to the boss.'

'You are speaking to him,' he said in a cool, impassive tone. 'I own Redstar.'

'You do?' Her composed expression slipped as she stared at him in amazement. 'But I thought——'

'I know what you thought,' Ryan cut in drily. 'You believed the hype they printed in the gutter Press. I'm surprised at you, Heather, really I am. I would have thought that working in the advertising world would teach you not to believe everything you see.' He smiled, but it was a smile devoid of amusement. 'I'm sorry to disappoint you, but I am not now, nor have I ever been, close to financial difficulties.'

'I'm not disappointed,' Heather answered steadily. 'Why should I be?'

'Why indeed?' he drawled, and his mouth twisted in a mocking smile. 'When Mrs Edwards seems to have done so well for herself.' His eyes moved to the gold band on her finger again, making her feel uneasy.

'Will you look at my portfolio?' she asked him directly, trying to swing the conversation back to business.

His eyes flickered briefly over the file in front of him and then back to her. 'You work for Craven's,' he murmured smoothly. 'I take it your husband owns the place?'

'No, he does not!' Heather snapped angrily.

'You do surprise me.' His glance slid lazily over her body. 'I would have thought only a lover would tolerate a member of staff who was shoddy enough to turn up late for an important appointment.'

Heather flinched. 'I . . . I know I was late and I'm sorry. Something unexpected held me up this morning.'

One dark eyebrow rose disdainfully. 'One thing about you in the past, Heather, you were always excellent at your job. Being married to Edwards has obviously taken the edge off your ambitions.'

'If you would care to look at my work I think you will discover quite the opposite,' she bit back sharply.

Again his eyes moved over the portfolio, but he made no attempt to touch it. 'I have no time this morning.' He glanced at his watch. 'My next appointment will be waiting for me. Besides, I employ somebody to sort through these things so I don't have to waste any time on the rubbish. Mr Adams was whom your appointment was with.'

'I don't deal in rubbish,' Heather told him calmly, while inside she was seething with raw rage. 'And I can assure you that my work will be far superior to anything that reaches you via Mr Adams. However, if you're not prepared to look at it, then that is just your loss.' She reached for the file, intending to pick it up and leave, but his hand shot out and caught hers before she had time to lift it. The contact of his skin against hers made blood rush madly through her veins; she felt hot and strangely disorientated.

'Not so fast, honey.' His lips curved in a half-smile and there was a grudging light of admiration in his deep blue eyes. 'You haven't lost that attractive fiery spirit, have you?' he said in a tight, rasping tone.

'When you want to climb high in the advertising world you need it.' She met his eyes steadily.

'That and an influential man.' He released her hand and sat back.

She recoiled at that almost as if he had physically struck her. Her dark lashes fell down on to the pallor of her skin, guarding her expressive eyes from his. 'Your opinion of me isn't very high, is it, Ryan?' Her voice was a mere whisper in the silence of the room. He made no reply and the silence stretched between them filled with a tension that was almost unbearable. Heather's hands clenched into tight fists as she tried to steel herself to meet his eyes.

'Will you look at my work or not?' Heather didn't know where she got the strength to say those words so calmly when all she wanted to do was hurl bitter recriminations at him. 'You and I are a thing of the past, Ryan, a closed issue, and I just want to forget all about it.' She finished with a rush, her eyes lifting towards his, a subliminal light of pleading in their shadowy depths.

He smiled at her, but it was a cold smile, one that was devoid of emotion. 'Of course you do,' he said quietly. 'Don't worry, Heather, I never confuse business with my private life.'

'So you will consider my work?' she pressed.

'I'll look at it,' he acknowledged with a nod of his dark head. Then, as she continued to look at him with uncertain eyes, he smiled, for a moment a brief look of indulgence on the ruggedly handsome face. 'With an unbiased perspective, I assure you,' he told her, a note of deep amusement in his voice. 'I am a businessman, Heather, first and foremost.'

'Yes, of course.' For a moment she felt incredibly stupid to think that his attitude would be anything other than a business one towards her. She should never have made that silly little speech about forgetting the past. Ryan Jameson would have more important things to dwell on than a little affair that had meant nothing to him. She stretched out one slender hand to open the portfolio for him.

'Leave it, Heather,' he ordered abruptly. 'I'll glance through it when I've got more time.'

She hesitated. 'But I really wanted to talk through my ideas with you. That way you——'

'If I think they're worth it, then we talk,' Ryan cut in forcefully.

'But I should really——'

'Heather, considering how inefficient you were at keeping your appointment this morning, I think you are being damned fortunate that I'm even going to glance at it. Don't press your luck,' he warned. 'Now be a good girl and get out of here so I can do some work.'

Heather glared at him. He was talking to her as if she were some errant schoolgirl, not a businesswoman who was head of her own department. Brown eyes clashed with blue for a moment before Heather's long lashes flickered down uncertainly. Perhaps he was right, she was lucky to get this far. Ryan wasn't the type of man who tolerated incompetence, and she was most probably privileged to have even got across the threshold of his office door.

'Very well, then, I'll leave it with you,' she said slowly.

'Wise choice,' he murmured with a sardonic smile.

Heather gritted her teeth and forced herself to smile back at him as she got up from her chair. 'I hope to hear from you soon, then.'

'Good day, Heather,' was his only reply as he opened a drawer in his desk and dropped her work into it with a resounding thud.

She stared at his arrogant, uncompromising face for a moment, her dark eyes glittering with anger, before nodding and walking gracefully towards the door.

Heather didn't remember anything about getting out of the Redstar building and hailing a taxi. She felt numb from the ordeal that she had just been through and she could hardly believe that she had just been sitting in Ryan's office, talking to a man that she had thought was out of her life forever.

A taxi pulled up for her and she climbed in, giving the Craven office address through a haze of confused thoughts. Would Ryan consider her work? she wondered. And if he did, if she was given the contract . . . what then? It would probably mean a lot more meetings like the one today. She would be forced into spending quite a lot of time with him. Suddenly the blood was draining away from her face as the reality of that situation finally struck home. Any involvement with Ryan Jameson could be absolutely devastating.

She leaned her head weakly back against the seat of the taxi. Ryan's attitude towards her had been arrogantly disdainful. He had taken real pleasure in tearing into her about her tardiness at keeping her appointment. What would he have said, she wondered, if she had told him the truth? That she had been late this morning because the child-minder had not arrived on time to take care of his daughter. That would really have made those blue eyes widen with shock!

CHAPTER TWO

AS USUAL the offices of Craven's advertising agency were hectic. The lively buzz that Heather usually found stimulating was grating on her over-stretched nerves today, and with a sigh she got up from her desk and closed her office door. No sooner had she sat down at her desk again than it was re-opened.

'Mr Craven wants to see you in his office, Mrs Edwards.' Liz, Heather's private secretary, announced and then, leaving the door open again, returned to her desk.

Sharp knives of tension stabbed through Heather and she stared down at her work without really seeing it. This was it, she felt sure that this was the moment she had been dreading ever since her meeting with Ryan Jameson last week. A summons to her boss's office could only mean one thing: Ryan had come to a decision about the advertising campaign. Robert Craven was either going to give her some sharp words about failing to gain the account, or he was going to congratulate her on bringing it in; she wished she knew which one she wanted it to be.

Slowly she rose from her desk, running a nervous slender hand down over an imaginary crease in the immaculate navy-blue suit. Then she made her way out and through the large open office where men were working over large drawing-boards. A few admiring glances followed her, but she was oblivious to them as she made her way out of the glass door and down the corridor to tap on Robert Craven's door.

'Ah, Heather, come in.' Robert Craven was beaming all over his round face, the small bright eyes alert and glittering with enthusiasm. Heather knew that look all too well, and her heart started to beat a rapid and wild tattoo.

'Well, congratulations, my dear. Ryan Jameson is very impressed with your ideas and he's coming in to discuss them with us.' He waved her towards the large swivel-chair facing him and Heather sat and nodded dumbly at him.

She had just brought in the largest contract of her career, probably the largest contract this company had ever handled, and she felt as if someone had just signed her death certificate. With a blinding flash she realised that she certainly didn't want this account—she didn't want anything to do with it. The price of being involved was just too high. Some things in life were more important than success and money, and one of those prime things was her daughter. If Ryan should ever find out about Sarah . . . The mere thought of it made her shudder. She knew Ryan Jameson well enough to know what his reaction would be.

'Heather, are you all right?' Robert stopped suddenly in mid-sentence to enquire, a small frown furrowing an already age-lined face.

She nodded. 'Yes, but I think I would prefer it if someone else handled this contract.'

'What?' Her boss's voice rose sharply by quite a few decibels and he stared at her as if she had gone mad. 'Do you mind telling me why?'

Heather hesitated. To say that she didn't want to do it because of personal reasons would not be a satisfactory explanation for Robert Craven. Work was the first and only priority to him, and little things like an individual's feelings would be swept quickly away as if she were just an irrational female. 'I just feel that someone else would do a better job than I would. Richard, for instance,' she told him, keeping her voice light and businesslike.

Robert gave a decisive snort of impatient disapproval. 'Heather, ever since you started work here you've been coming into my office trying to prove to me how much better your work is than anybody else's.' For a moment the anger on his face was replaced by a gleam of approval. 'The hell of it is, you've been right and I've always known it. I don't know why you're suddenly starting to backtrack on me now, Heather, but I'm not going to stand for it.' He tapped some of her work that was lying before him on the huge marble and chrome desk. 'It's your concepts and your hard work that have brought in the Redstar account, and you are going to follow it through and there's an end to it. Besides . . .' Robert's beady eyes narrowed on her. '. . . I don't think Ryan Jameson would agree to anyone else's handling the campaign. He's not the type of man to settle for second best. So, unless you want the contract to fly out of the window, you're stuck with it, young lady.'

Robert pulled some of the sheets of paper on his desk towards him in a decisive, no-nonsense way. 'Now, let's get the men from accounts up here and make a start before Mr Jameson arrives.'

Heather stared helplessly at the iron-grey head of hair that was bent over her work. It was obvious that she was going to get nowhere with her boss. Unless she gave in her notice it looked as if there was no other means of escape, and that was far too drastic a measure. Or was it? Maybe desperate situations called for equally severe solutions.

'Run your eye over these, will you, Heather?' Her

boss handed her over a stack of papers and she absent-mindedly tried to concentrate on them. She must not let Ryan Jameson destroy her life again; she must be strong and try to ride out this storm.

She remembered the first time she had ever seen Ryan. He had strolled into the offices of Harper's ad agency as if he owned the place, and a few weeks later he had owned it. Heather's lips twisted in a derisive smile. Ryan was a collector, he collected businesses just as some people collected stamps, and he always turned them into thriving success stories. He had a brilliant business mind and he was a computer whiz. Usually the first thing he did when he acquired a company was to install the latest and the best in computer technology, and from that point on it seemed he had the Midas touch—everything he so much as glanced at turned to gold.

Heather had been a very junior member of staff at Harper's. Twenty-one and fresh out of college, she hadn't thought that a man like Ryan Jameson would have even noticed she existed. She had adored him from the first moment she had set eyes on him, probably just as all the other female members of staff had. He had the kind of magnetic attractiveness that instantly made a woman's heartbeat increase dramatically. If he had so much as glanced in Heather's direction she had grown weak at the knees.

When the initial changes had been made in the business Ryan had installed a manager, and his visits to the agency grew few and far between. Then one bright morning he walked in, came straight to her desk and told her to get her coat. For one horrific moment Heather thought she was being fired. Then quite calmly he enquired if she had any preference as to which restaurant he took her to for lunch. He behaved as coolly and arrogantly as if they had been having lunch together since the beginning of time. She was astounded, and in a state of shock lifted her bag and picked up her coat, only vaguely aware of the excited buzz of interest and the envious glances from the other women.

He took her to an exclusive restaurant and talked to her in an easy, friendly manner. He asked her opinion of the changes he had made at work and what she thought of the new manager. She answered in a stilted voice; she was very much in awe of him.

When Ryan signalled the waiter to bring over the dessert trolley, Heather glanced nervously at her watch. 'I don't think I have time for anything else,' she said in a worried tone. 'I only have an hour for lunch.'

Ryan gave one of his attractive smiles. 'That is one of the advantages of dining with the boss—it doesn't matter about the time.'

'But Mr Neilson will be expecting me back, sir.' The sir just slipped out. She had been agonising over what to call him all through lunch. He used her Christian name with familiar ease, but she just couldn't bring herself to do the same, so she had avoided calling him anything.

One dark eyebrow rose. 'Leave me to worry about Neilson,' he told her drily. 'And you can dispense with the sir bit, it's far too casual a title for my liking. You can call me Ryan.' He grinned at her, but she still couldn't relax. She refused anything from the dessert trolley and ordered a coffee instead.

'Not worried about your figure, surely?' Ryan frowned.

'No.' Heather's eyes met his and suddenly her old confidence returned. 'I'm worried about why my boss seems to have taken such a sudden interest in me,' she told him steadily. 'If you wanted to discuss business you could have asked your manager out to lunch.'

'True.' He smiled. 'But then Brian Neilson isn't nearly as good-looking as you are.'

'There are plenty of good-looking women in the office. Women who are in higher positions than mine,' she couldn't stop herself from replying.

'Yes, there are.' Ryan smiled a gentle, indulgent smile that did strange things to her blood-pressure. 'But why should I ask any of them when it's you that I want?'

And Heather had wanted him. Even now, all these years later, she couldn't deny that fact.

'So tell me a little about yourself,' Ryan invited, leaning back in his chair and studying her through brilliantly blue eyes.

'There isn't much to tell really.' She smiled.

'I don't believe that for a moment,' Ryan said, shaking his head. 'I know all about your working life, how good you are at your job and how highly qualified you are. But what do you do outside work? Have you got a serious boyfriend?'

'Nobody serious, no.' Heather smiled again. 'I've lived alone for the last four years since my mother died. I have a small flat not far from work.'

'And what about your father, where is he?' Ryan probed.

Heather's dark eyes clouded momentarily, and she shrugged. 'I have no idea. He left home when I was eight and I never saw him again.'

He leaned across and covered her small slender hand with his. The gentle pressure of his skin against hers made her flush hotly and she babbled on in confusion. 'And I like going to the theatre and concerts and listening to quiet romantic music.'

'Would you like to listen to some quiet romantic

music this afternoon?' he asked, his voice deep and husky. 'We could go back to my apartment.'

She shook her head, lowering her eyelashes to hide her eyes from him. She knew exactly what he was inviting, but as much as she might be tempted there was no way she would sleep with him. Maybe she was old-fashioned in her outlook, but she had always held the idea in her heart that she would never give herself to a man unless she was deeply in love with him.

'Well, we're still on for the theatre and a concert, I hope?' he asked in such a grave voice that she had to smile.

Ryan had brought sunshine and laughter into her life. In the weeks that followed that first lunch he had courted her relentlessly. Heather had always felt the term 'courted' was a rather archaic description of relationships nowadays, but Ryan had taught her the true meaning of the word and she had loved every minute. He wined and dined her, sent her flowers and romantic gifts, always took her to the best places and made her feel as if she was the most special person in his life.

Heather was enough of a realist not to fall for the glitter and enchantment of being Ryan Jameson's girlfriend. It wasn't the sophisticated places he brought her to or his presents that had swept Heather off her feet, it was the person she had glimpsed behind that urbane veneer of the tough businessman. She had fallen for a man who was tender-hearted and sentimental, a man who could make her laugh and cry with equal ease. Looking back now, she could realise that had just been his clever strategy to win her over and get her into his bed. It had certainly had the desired effect; she had fallen for him and fallen hard.

Ryan Jameson had awakened a passionate side of her

nature she had never known existed. Exactly six weeks after that first lunch date Ryan had asked her to move into his apartment on Park Avenue.

'No strings,' he told her firmly before she could make any reply. She didn't take long to think about it; she was completely under his spell by that time and deeply in love. She would have agreed to anything that meant getting a little closer to him.

So early one Saturday morning he collected her from her small rented flat and she was transported into a world of luxury and elegance. No longer did she have to worry about finances and whether she had enough money left over at the end of the month to buy a new dress. Ryan showered her with presents, a new wardrobe full of the most expensive clothes, beautiful jewellery. He gave her more than she really wanted, but in her naïveté she presumed he spoilt her because he loved her. Little had she guessed that she had become just another one of his possessions, bought and paid for.

'Heather, are you all right?' Robert Craven's voice seemed to be coming from a great distance and she stared at her boss for a moment before coming sharply back to the present.

'Yes, sorry, Robert, were you saying something?' she asked breathlessly.

'Yes. What do you think of those figures?' he enquired with a frown.

'Er . . .' Helplessly Heather stared down at the sheets of paper in front of her, realising that she hadn't taken in anything about them, so deep had been her reminiscences. Mercifully at that moment there was a tap on the door and two men from the accounts department came in, distracting her boss's attention, and the question was forgotten.

Heather forced herself to concentrate for the next hour, firmly pushing all thoughts of Ryan from her mind. But as the time of his arrival grew imminent she could feel her nerves starting to prickle and her head starting to pound angrily, as if a hundred little men were inside her skull hammering away.

At the first opportunity she excused herself and went quickly back to her office to get some pain-killers from her handbag. She felt a little better as soon as she swallowed two, and she got out a small mirror from her bag to repair her lipstick. She needed a few minutes to gather herself together before she could face Ryan.

For a moment she stared at her reflection in the mirror. Her skin looked far too pale, her eyes dark and shadowed. Almost like old times, she thought grimly as she snapped the compact shut. A few weeks after she first moved in with Ryan she had spent a lot of her days looking like this, and she had been tired—so tired that some days it had been a real effort just to keep her eyes open.

At first she hadn't realised what was wrong with her. She had put the sick feeling down to nerves. She had been going through a tough phase at work, and then there was Ryan. She had noticed a definite cooling in his attitude towards her. He had seemed to be preoccupied with something, and whatever it was he hadn't wanted to discuss it with her.

She leaned her head back against the chair and stared up at the ceiling. That was the point when everything had gone wrong and her life had changed from one of idealistic happiness into a nightmare.

It had started with a small episode at work one morning. She hadn't been feeling very well and had left her desk to go down to the rest-room for a moment. Before she could push the door open she had heard her name mentioned and had hesitated. It seemed that a few female members of staff were having quite a conversation about her relationship with Ryan.

'Do you think it's going to last?' one girl was asking, and Heather heard the grating laugh of her immediate superior Lyn Perry.

'Of course it's not going to last. Anyone can see he's tired of her already. Word has it he's seeing someone else.' Lyn lowered her voice to a conspiring whisper. 'I've also heard that Ryan is having some financial troubles; it seems he's selling off some of his companies.'

Heather turned and left them to their gossip. Heat rose in a nauseous wave from her stomach to her head, and she ran towards the Ladies', barely making it in time. Afterwards, as she leaned her head weakly against one of the washbasins and splashed her face with cool water, she tried to dismiss what she had heard as utter nonsense. None of those girls knew Ryan Jameson as she did. He loved her, she was almost sure he did. She studied her reflection in the mirror in front of her. She looked dreadful, her skin had a deathly pallor and her eyes and hair lacked their usual lustre. Did Ryan love her? she wondered miserably. Suddenly she felt like crying, which was nothing unusual just lately. She had been very tearful over the last few weeks, most unlike her normal sunny nature.

'You're going to have to pull yourself together, Heather Jennings,' she told herself firmly. 'And if you're unsure of Ryan's feelings you are going to have to ask him straight.' She took a comb out of her handbag and pulled it roughly through her hair. There would be no beating around the bush for her; she would come straight to the point. Do you love me, Ryan?

It wasn't as easy as she had envisaged. When she got back to the apartment that night Ryan had left on business for a few days. And when she next saw him she had discovered something that changed everything. She was pregnant.

She agonised over what to do. What would Ryan's reaction be to the fact that he was going to become a father? Anger? Yes, most probably. He had left the matter of contraception to her. He had discussed it with her quite candidly right back at the beginning, and had asked her what she would prefer to use. She had been highly embarrassed by the conversation and had mumbled that she would see her doctor, and she had. She didn't even think she had forgotten to take any of those pills. But she must have. It was her own stupid fault and she was terrified to tell Ryan. What if he thought she was trying to trap him into marriage? He could end up hating her. Suddenly she remembered his words to her before she moved in. 'No strings,' he had said.

Ryan took her out to dinner a couple of days after he got back and it was then that he dropped his own bombshell.

She had been doing silent battle with herself all night, trying to decide whether she should tell him or not, when suddenly he pushed aside his plate, making her realise that he too had only been toying with his food. She had hardly noticed the strained silence during the meal; she had been so preoccupied with her own thoughts. Now as she stared at him across the table she was suddenly petrified. This was it, she knew it. He was going to tell her that he didn't want to continue with their relationship.

'You know, don't you?' he murmured softly across the table, and she bit down sharply on her trembling lips, her eyes wide and haunted.

'I'm sorry, Heather. I've been meaning to tell you for a while.'

'Who . . . who is she?' Heather's voice was a mere husky whisper.

'Who?' For a moment he frowned, then his brow cleared. 'So you even know that.' He shook his head. 'And I thought it was such a well-kept secret.' He signalled the waiter to bring him another drink before he continued. 'Your job will be safe, Heather. There is no need to worry about that.'

'I wasn't,' she answered dully. It had never crossed her mind that Ryan would fire her from her job if their relationship didn't work out. He wasn't that type of man.

'Brian Neilson has bought Harper's, so things should continue much as usual,' he continued briskly.

'You've sold Harper's?' Heather asked in startled amazement.

'Yes, it's had to go, along with all my British-based companies for the time being. I'm concentrating solely on America for a while—there's a very large computer company I am negotiating for. I've decided to channel everything into it.' His eyes narrowed on her. 'I thought you knew. I assumed that was the reason you've been so preoccupied recently.'

'I . . . I suspected something,' Heather hedged, looking away from the bright intensity of those blue eyes. 'And who . . . who is the woman? she asked stiffly.

'You mean Annabel Rothstar? She's twenty-one years of age and she owns one of the largest computer companies in the States.' He noted her raised eyebrow with a grin. 'Daddy has just died and left it all to her,' he explained. 'She's desperate to sell it, and I'm very anxious to buy it, but unfortunately I have run into some complications.'

'And are you having an affair with her?' Heather's voice trembled alarmingly as she asked the question.

Ryan's face darkened angrily. 'Don't be ridiculous. You know how I feel about you.'

She shook her head and a lump came into her throat. 'No, I don't Ryan. How do you feel?'

For a moment there was silence; she could feel her heart thudding painfully against her ribs as she waited for his answer.

'I'm not in a position to be able to make any commitment to you—if that's what you mean,' he said bluntly, and then reached for her hand. 'I have a lot of pressures on me at the moment, Heather. I have to go to the States next week and I will be staying there for quite some time. I'm going to start looking for a house over there as soon as possible. When things are more settled, then we can decide about our relationship—perhaps you would like to come out to me or I'll come back.' He shrugged. 'It's hard to say how things will work out just at this moment. Try to understand.'

Heather nodded bleakly. She understood all right. Ryan didn't love her—if he had he would have wanted her to go to the States with him and they would have chosen a home where they would live together. 'Yes, I understand,' she murmured, trying to swallow down that painful lump in her throat, and she understood that there was no way now that she could tell him about their child.

She stayed with him in the apartment right up to the time of his departure, and she despised herself for that weakness. She should have packed her bags and left him the moment he made his feelings for her plain, but she just didn't have the strength to do it. She held on to him tightly during those last few nights when they were together, loving the feel of his skin beneath her fingertips, resting her face against his broad chest. The thought of his leaving her and going all those thousands of miles away terrified her. How was she going to manage without him? She loved him so much.

She couldn't help the tears that rolled down her cheek one night, and he cradled her gently against him. 'Don't cry, sweetheart. I promise it won't be for long.'

She sat on the edge of the bed the following morning and watched as he threw a few last-minute things into a suitcase. Her heart squeezed into a throbbing hard knot in her chest as she tried to control a well of emotion that made her want to scream and plead with him not to go.

'I'll come with you to the airport,' she managed to say calmly.

He looked at her pale face and the dark shadows beneath her eyes and shook his head.

'Please, Ryan. I'm a glutton for punishment. I want to see you walk through those gates.'

For a moment he hesitated, then he agreed, shutting his cases with a decisive click.

'Ryan, are you having financial difficulties?' she asked him suddenly.

He turned slowly, his eyes narrowing on her. 'What makes you ask that?'

She shrugged. How could she say that she was desperately searching her mind to find some reason to excuse the way he was leaving her, something she could understand? 'I overheard some people talking about it, that's all.'

'You shouldn't listen to idle gossip,' was all he said in reply.

They travelled to Heathrow airport in silence. Ryan held her hand and squeezed it gently. She looked at his face—there was a faraway expression in his blue eyes, and she knew that his mind was already on the business ahead of him. The love of Ryan's life was his career, she knew that; it was the reason that he was so successful.

They sat in the departure lounge and had a coffee together. Every mouthful seemed to stick in Heather's throat. How was she going to get through this pregnancy on her own? Just say she never saw Ryan again—would her child never know its father? She placed an instinctively protective hand down on to the still flat plane of her stomach.

Ryan noticed the gesture and frowned. 'Are you all right?'

She stared at him for a moment—she wanted so much to tell him—then she gave a shaky smile. 'It's this airport coffee.' She wrinkled her small nose. 'It tastes more like acorns than anything else.'

He grinned. 'Yes, dreadful, stuff. Count yourself lucky you won't be having the meal on the plane—that will probably be worse.'

Heather stared down at her hands. 'I don't feel very lucky,' she murmured softly, but he didn't hear her because at that moment his flight was called.

'Well, this is it, honey.' He smiled at her and got up. 'Come on, you can walk me to the gate.'

He slipped an arm around her waist as they walked. 'I hope you are going to take good care of yourself while I'm away.'

'I'll take my vitamins every day,' she managed to answer flippantly.

'Good girl.' They stopped by the gate and he turned her towards him, taking her into his arms. His lips came down on hers in a long, lingering kiss. When he made to pull away from her she clung to him, panic suddenly filling her body. She couldn't bear him to leave her; she couldn't let him go. She looked up into those midnight-blue eyes. 'Ryan, I . . . there's something I haven't told you.' She blurted the words out.

'Oh?' He frowned and held her away from him so that he could see her face clearly. 'What is it?'

Sanity returned sharply. How could she tell him, here of all places? What did she expect him to do about it—refuse to leave her? Or was she hoping that he would take her with him? Either way it would be emotional blackmail. He had already made it clear to her that he didn't want any commitments, and wasn't a child one of the biggest commitments you made in life? If she told him now he would end up resenting her or, worse, hating her. She shook her head helplessly. 'It . . . it doesn't matter. It can wait.'

'Sure?' Those eyes pierced into her and she nodded.

Then she was in his arms again for the last time before he turned and walked out of her life. She watched him go, tears blurring his tall, dark frame.

It was as she turned and walked back through the crowded airport that the first pains started. To begin with they were just a dull, throbbing ache. But, as she hailed a taxi and got in, they turned into sharp, vicious thrusts that made her gasp in pain.

'Are you all right, miss?' The taxi-driver turned to look at her tear-stained face as she gave another low moan of anguish.

She shook her head. 'No . . . I . . . I think you had better take me to a hospital.'

Someone was tapping on Heather's office door. Horrified, she brushed a trembling hand over her face, trying to wipe away the tears that were streaming down it in never-ending rivulets. Her blood ran cold at the thought of someone seeing her in this state.

'Heather, I just——' Richard Craven, the boss's son popped his head around the door, a bright smile on his face that faded at the sight of her. 'What on earth is the matter?' He came in quickly to crouch down beside her chair, looking at her with a concerned light in his steady grey eyes. 'Has someone upset you, Heather? Because if they have I'll——'

'No, nothing like that, Richard,' she cut in hastily, desperately trying to stem the flood of tears and feeling very foolish. 'I'm just not feeling very well, that's all.' It wasn't a complete lie—she did feel awful.

'I see,' he murmured, and took out a linen handkerchief from the top pocket of his stylish suit to hand to her.

'Thanks.' She gave him a trembling smile, noting the perplexed look on his handsome face. No wonder he was bewildered, she thought, cringing inwardly. Heather Edwards was always in control, always calm and collected, no matter what the crisis. It was a veneer that she had carefully promoted over the years at Craven's in order to keep her distance from her fellow workers. Now here she was crying her heart out! Richard was probably wondering if the ice maiden had finally melted. Her lips twisted wryly—she knew that some of the men in the office had dubbed her the 'ice maiden' because of her aloof attitude and the way she always refused any dates.

'I feel a lot better now,' she told him in a firmer tone, and handed his handkerchief back. 'I think it was a slight migraine.'

'Would you like me to take you home?' he offered quickly.

She shook her head and grinned. 'Robert would have

a fit if he'd heard you say that.'

'Probably.' He grinned back at her. 'I only popped in to congratulate you on the Redstar account. How about going out to dinner tonight to celebrate——?' His voice dropped to a low husky tone.

'Perhaps I should come back later when you're not so busy,' a cool voice from the doorway interrupted, making them turn with a start.

Ryan Jameson was standing just inside the room, his eyes like cool chips of ice as they rested on Heather's flushed countenance and the intimate way Richard was leaning close towards her.

'No . . . no, we're not busy.' Richard struggled to his feet, looking flustered and embarrassed under Ryan's hard scrutiny. 'Actually, I was just leaving.' He shot an apologetic glance down at Heather, before moving quickly from the room.

There was a strained silence for a moment after he left. Heather shifted uncomfortably under Ryan's harsh stare and wondered how on earth he had managed to walk unannounced into her office. Where the hell was Liz?

'That, I take it, was your husband?' Ryan asked in a glacial voice.

Heather's eyebrows shot up in startled amazement. 'He certainly is not. That is Robert Craven's son Richard. He is merely a colleague.'

Ryan walked slowly towards her. He had the dangerous look of a predator about to pounce and Heather felt a sudden quiver of apprehension stir inside her.

'And does your husband know you are having an affair with a mere colleague?' he asked contemptuously.

CHAPTER THREE

'HOW dare you surmise about my personal life?' Heather rasped furiously. 'And, for your information, my husband is dead.'

Strange how easily that lie came to her lips when she was by nature such an honest person. Probably it was because she had told it so many times over the years. She was an expert now at murmuring that she was a widow and putting just the right amount of sorrow and grief into her expressive brown eyes to discourage further questioning about her supposed husband.

Unfortunately the grief-stricken eyes that she turned up towards him didn't have the same effect as they normally did. Instead of the usual brief word of sympathy before the subject was tactfully dropped, Ryan seemed to home in on it.

'How long ago did he die?' he asked, his eyes raking over her, missing nothing.

'A few years ago,' she answered vaguely. Discomfited, she moved further back into her chair. She didn't want him prying into her life, especially this area of it. This was what she was most afraid of.

'You can't have been married long,' Ryan went on, unconcerned by her obvious distress.

'No.' Her slender hands clenched into tight fists as they rested on her desk. She was unaware of the fact until she noticed his eyes move towards them. Immediately she forced herself to relax. 'So you liked my work, Ryan,' she managed to say coolly, deliberately changing the subject towards business and injecting an aloof, impersonal note into the proceedings.

His firm mouth relaxed fractionally. 'As you so rightly predicted, Heather, it was the best I could find. But then I've never been able to fault your work.' He gave quiet emphasis to that last statement, making her eyes narrow angrily. What was that supposed to mean? That he couldn't fault her work, only her? The man had an arrogant nerve, talking to her like that.

Before she had time to make a reply, her office door swung open and Robert Craven came in, closely followed by the two men from the accounts department. 'Ah, good, you found Heather.' Robert came to stand next to Ryan, looking like a dwarf next to the other man's powerful build. 'I've got all those figures ready for you to look over now, Mr Jameson.' He placed some papers down on to the desk. 'And my accountants are here in case you want to ask any questions.'

'Yes, well, before we go through the cost of the campaign there are a few more important items I would like to discuss,' Ryan told him easily.

'But of course.' For once in his life Robert Craven was looking a little flustered as he strove to accommodate this important client. 'Where would you like to start?'

Heather bit on her lower lip, for some reason feeling irritated by her boss's respectful attitude towards Ryan. Why was it that everyone always fawned around that man? Was it his money? His power? She glanced up at him and met that steel-like gaze. No, probably that aura of commanding strength, she decided quickly. Ryan Jameson could be wholly formidable.

'Perhaps Heather will run through her ideas for me in greater detail?'

Heather nodded and waited while the men seated themselves in comfortable chairs opposite her before she began. She went through her plans for the campaign in a crisp, confident voice, but inside she was feeling very self-conscious. She wished Ryan wouldn't watch her so intently. His blue eyes seemed so sharp, all-seeing, all-consuming. It would be hard to hide anything from such a man. She shivered and finished what she was saying in a rush. Her long slim hands trembled slightly as she rearranged her work into neat piles before her. 'Is there anything you would like to ask me, Mr Jameson?' she forced herself to say.

One dark brow rose in an almost mocking way. 'There is a great deal I would like to ask you, Heather,' he drawled, and again there was that underlying note to his words that made her nerves clench with tension. 'But as I don't have a lot of time, I'll just run through a few basic points that bother me.' He proceeded to ask about a few things that she had only mentioned briefly, and she expanded on them in greater detail for him, marvelling at the ease with which he absorbed everything without even taking down a note.

He nodded when she had finished. 'Well, it certainly is a brilliant concept. It outlines just what modern computers will do for today's businessman, and it's catchy too. I think it will be very successful for us.' He pursed his lips slightly and Heather could almost hear his mind ticking over as he thought some more about her ideas. 'Are you thinking of using any well-known personalities to do the advertisement?'

'I haven't looked into that aspect yet,' Heather admitted.

'Mmm . . .' Ryan drummed his fingers on her desk-top as he thought about it some more. 'I just might be able to get Annabel Rothstar to do it. She would be perfect because not only did she once to own my company but she's a very well-known personality. She's not bad to look at either,' he tacked on, his mouth slanting in a grin.

Heather didn't return that amused smile, she just stared at him. Her heart seemed to have plunged somewhere down into her stomach. 'I don't think that is such a good idea,' she told him in a cold, stony voice.

'Why ever not?' Robert Craven intervened quickly. 'Seeing that gorgeous woman would certainly capture a man's attention. I think it could work.'

'It's not just the men's attention that we want to capture. Besides, we want people to be looking at the computers, not the person in front of them,' Heather told him, but even as she spoke she wondered if most of her objections to the woman were based on personal reasons rather than anything else. Her heart was thumping madly, and, oddly, she felt a twinge of real dislike towards a woman whom she had never met.

'I agree that we are aiming towards the businesswoman as well as the man, but I think Annabel will appeal to both. She will give the advertisement a certain class without detracting from the computer,' Ryan said briskly.

Heather strove desperately to get her personal feeling out of the way. Her one concern here should be a professional one; nothing else should influence her. 'I'm . . . I'm not sure about this at all. I think it will have to be given a lot more thought,' she mumbled at last.

'Well, Annabel might not be free to do the advertisement for us anyway, so the whole thing is hypothetical at the moment.' Ryan's blue eyes narrowed on her. 'I'm giving a house party this weekend at my home in Cheshire. Annabel will be there, so perhaps you would like to come over and we'll talk to her together.'

Heather's dark eyes widened and her delicate skin visibly paled. There was no way on this earth that she would even contemplate spending a weekend at Ryan's country house, meeting his mistress! The man must be completely insensitive.

'I'm afraid that I have already made plans for this weekend.' Her voice held a faint quiver of alarm. As well as everything else she couldn't leave Sarah. She had never stayed away from her overnight—it was bad enough being separated from her during the day.

'Oh, come now, Heather, I'm sure it's nothing you can't change.' Robert gave her a hard stare, willing her to comply with this new important client.

'I'm afraid it is,' Heather answered firmly.

Robert's mouth tightened into a thin line. It was an ominous sign—one that meant her boss was about to tread the war-path. 'I think, Heather, that you should rearrange your plans just this once,' he told her in a no-nonsense tone.

'Maybe Heather's date is more important to her,' Ryan remarked drily, making Heather's cool façade crumble a little, and her eyes flashed fire at him.

'I really can't see the point to my meeting Ms Rothstar. Besides, I would find it difficult to get over to Cheshire on a Friday evening, as I have no car.'

'That's easily solved. I'll pick you up,' Ryan suggested easily. 'And there is a point, Heather. I am giving this company a very big contract; I expect the best in return. That means your time as well as your expertise. If you are not prepared to give that . . .' he stood up, his manner cool as he glanced around the room and finally let his eyes rest back on Heather '. . . I can always take the account elsewhere.'

'Now there's no need to be hasty!' Robert Craven jumped up and Heather could see him palpably blanch. 'You will of course have the best advertisement campaign that money can buy in terms of both expertise and time.'

'I'm glad to hear it,' Ryan drawled, glancing at his watch. 'I have no more time to discuss things further, but I'll ring later in the week to arrange picking you up, Heather.' Then with a curt nod to everyone he left the room.

Heather stared at the door, totally dumbfounded. This was turning into a nightmare.

The two men from accounts mumbled something and left quickly behind him. Heather wasn't surprised they had made such a speedy departure when she turned and looked at Robert's face. It had turned a very nasty shade of red.

'What the hell do you think you are playing at?' he demanded of her furiously. 'Do you realise that you nearly lost us that account?'

'He was probably bluffing,' Heather answered grimly. 'And he has no right whatsoever to make demands like that.'

'Heather, for the amount of money that man will be paying us I can assure you he has the right to ask the whole office to go down to his home.' He stared at her for a moment and there was a strained silence. 'Look, I realise you must have your reasons for behaving in so out of character a manner,' he muttered suddenly, 'but for God's sake get your act together. This contract is very important to the company. It might mean all the difference between our sinking or swimming.'

* * *

Should she start looking for another job? Heather wondered despondently as she sat at her desk on Friday afternoon. Did she want to change jobs? The answer came back very clearly; no, she did not. She liked working at Craven's. This job had helped her build up her self-esteem after it had been at an all-time low; it had helped her through a very difficult black period of her life. She even liked Robert Craven—although he was a tough businessman, he had always been fair to her and she respected him.

She thought again about his comments concerning the company. Were they really in financial difficulties? Heather hadn't noticed any slackening in her workload. Maybe other parts of the department were not as busy as they should be. If that was the case, didn't she have an obligation to Robert and the company to try her best for the Redstar contract?

Liz popped her head around the door. 'Mr Craven says you can leave early if you want, Mrs Edwards.'

Heather's eyebrows rose. Robert had never let her finish ahead of time before. Somehow it seemed to denote just how important this weekend was to him.

Heather started to clear her desk. There was no point sitting here any longer anyway. She had hardly done a stroke of work all day. Her thoughts had all been centred around Ryan and the alarming fact that he was picking her up tonight to spend a night at his home. A nervous flutter stirred inside her as she put on her coat. She felt almost sick with apprehension.

It was a beautiful day outside. The sky was an electric blue, and everything was sharp and crisp although bitterly cold. Heather walked briskly towards the bus-stop and then on impulse stopped to gaze in the windows of a large department store at some of the latest dress fashions.

Should she buy a new dress for the party tonight? she wondered. She didn't possess anything that was very exciting. Most of her clothes were smart and businesslike, reflecting the fact that most of her outings were in connection with her career—which was the way she wanted it. Her lips curved wryly as she remembered how she had turned down Richard's invitation only a few days ago. Richard was a very nice person, but not someone that she wanted to get involved with. Come to that, she didn't really want to be involved with anybody; she had been hurt too badly in the past to want to risk her emotions again. Besides, she didn't think she would be capable of loving anyone the way she had loved Ryan. She sighed impatiently. Ryan was an arrogant swine; she must have been crazy to fall for him in the first place. He had rung the office this morning and had coolly informed her that he would pick her up at seven, without so much as checking with her that it was all right. To make matters worse, he had already got her address from Robert.

Heather glared at the beautiful fashions in the window and turned angrily away from them. No, she damn well wasn't going to waste time buying a new dress—why should she? She had no wish to impress Ryan, and she certainly was not in competition with Annabel Rothstar.

She moved further down the pavement, passing a window filled with children's toys. A large rag doll caught her eye. It was exquisite, dressed in Victorian clothes with big blue eyes that seemed to cry out for someone to buy it. Sarah would love it, Heather thought immediately, and it was her birthday next week.

It was warm inside the store and already they were

playing Christmas carols, making Heather realise how near it was to that festive season.

She purchased the doll and then wandered around the toy department, wondering if she should do some Christmas shopping while she was here. She was usually dashing around at the last minute the week before.

She noticed a young couple in front of her, the woman heavily pregnant, her arm linked through her husband's as they wandered around. For one crazy second she felt a pang of sadness as she watched them. If only things had been different—if only Ryan had loved her as much as she loved him they could have been a real family. How wonderful it would have been if Ryan could have shared the magic and excitement of Christmas with his daughter.

She turned away from the rows of toys and glittering tinsel, her eyes blurring suddenly. What on earth was the matter with her? she wondered furiously. Sarah and she were a real family, they didn't need Ryan or anyone else in their lives. And as for Ryan's sharing anything with either of them! That had to be the joke of the year. The only thing Ryan understood was control and possession.

Sarah was painting at the kitchen table when Heather arrived home. She was dressed in denim dungarees and a fluffy blue jumper. She looked warm and cuddly, her cheeks flushed, her eyes bright sapphire-blue.

'Mumma, you're home!' She scrambled quickly off the chair and hurled herself into Heather's arms.

'Steady on, you're getting a bit big for that now.' Heather smiled as she swung her up easily and kissed her. She felt hot and Heather placed a hand against her forehead in concern. 'I think you've got a temperature, young lady,' she said, turning questioning eyes towards Susan who was starting to prepare tea.

'Yes, she's been like that all day,' she confirmed. 'I think it's probably just a chill, something similar to what I had last week.'

Heather felt a twinge of panic. Of all times for Sarah to be ill, it would have to be when she was leaving her. 'Perhaps I should cancel this business trip. If Sarah's not well I'd rather not go,' she murmured, her forehead creasing with worried lines.

'Oh, no, don't do that.' Susan shook her head. 'It's just a slight cold. She'll probably be all right after a good night's sleep.'

'Susan made me drink some awful-tasting medicine,' Sarah told her mother dolefully, wrinkling her small nose in disgust.

'Well, it's just to make you feel better, darling.' Heather smiled.

'I feel all right.' The little girl wriggled to get down from Heather's arms. 'Look at the picture I've painted for you, Mumma.'

'It's beautiful,' Heather enthused, glancing at the bright colourful daubs on the white paper. 'When you go to real school you'll probably be the best artist in the class.'

Sarah nodded her head in solemn agreement before picking up her brush to add a few more yellow strokes.

Heather watched her closely. She didn't look too ill, and whatever it was that was ailing her didn't seem to be affecting her too badly. Perhaps it would be ridiculous to cancel the trip to Cheshire. 'Do you think you'll be all right while I'm away, Sarah?' she asked cautiously.

The little girl stopped what she was doing for a

minute to stare up at her with wide, enquiring eyes. 'When are you going?'

'Tonight. Remember I told you all about it yesterday?' Heather said gently.

Sarah nodded. 'Oh, yes, I'll be all right.' She swung her attention back to her art. 'I'm going to paint hundreds and hundreds of pictures for you while you're gone.'

Heather gave Susan a rueful smile. 'Looks as if I'm the only one who's upset about going.'

'Well, it is the first time you've left her overnight,' Susan answered with sympathy. 'But she'll be fine. I'll take good care of her.'

Heather nodded. 'Well, I think I'll go and take a quick shower and throw a few things into a case.' She forced a bright note into her voice and ruffled Sarah's hair before turning to go back out into the hall.

God, she didn't want to go, she thought as she tucked the bag with Sarah's doll in it towards the back of her wardrobe away from beady eyes. For a moment she sat back on her bed and stared at the rows of clothes facing her. She didn't want to spend any time with Ryan, and she didn't want to leave Sarah.

She knew she was a little over-protective about her daughter—maybe it was because she was a single parent and she felt that all the responsibility rested squarely on her shoulders, or perhaps it was the fact that she had come so very near to losing Sarah . . .

'You're going to have to take things very easy from here on, young lady,' the doctor told her sternly.

Heather nodded mutely, praying that he was going to discharge her. She had never spent any time in a hospital before, and one night had seemed like a very frightening eternity.

'Complete bed rest,' the doctor went on.

She lifted wide, startled eyes at that. 'But my work! I've got to——'

'Work will have to wait,' the doctor cut in impatiently. 'You have to rest, otherwise . . .' His voice trailed off ominously.

'Otherwise I might lose the baby?' Heather finished for him, cold fear rising up inside her. She hadn't realised until this moment just how much she wanted this baby. The thought that she might lose it was too painful to even think about.

'It's a very real possibility.' He nodded, then, seeing her pale skin blanch even whiter, he went on gently, 'But if you follow all my instructions there's no reason why you shouldn't have a perfectly healthy baby.'

When Heather returned to the apartment she had shared with Ryan later that evening, she felt emotionally and physically drained. It felt like a lifetime ago that she had seen Ryan leave at the airport, instead of only yesterday morning.

The phone was ringing incessantly as she let herself in the front door, and she forced herself not to rush to pick it up. It would probably be Brian Neilson wanting to know why she hadn't turned up for work.

'Where the hell have you been?' Ryan's voice thundered down the phone, furiously angry. 'I've been trying to get hold of you since the early hours of this morning.'

His tone made her feel even more wretchedly ill and frightened and her temper snapped. 'I've been out,' she told him sharply.

'Out where?' he demanded.

'At an all-night party.' Her voice dripped with

sarcasm. 'And it's none of your damned business where I've been. You don't own me.'

There was silence for a moment while he digested this. She had never spoken to him like that before. 'Yes, I do,' he answered calmly. 'You are the woman who has been living at my apartment for the last few months, the woman I held in my arms only yesterday. You are my possession,' he told her grimly. 'Now where the hell have you been all night?'

'I told you,' she said dully.

'At a party.' His voice was formidable. 'Who with?'

Her mind had gone blank for a few seconds. 'With a friend.' She stumbled over the words.

'My God, Heather, it hasn't taken you long to replace me, has it? To think that I was taken in by those dark pain-filled eyes yesterday!'

Her anger started to melt away and tears slowly trickled down her cheeks. 'It's not like that.' Her voice was low and pleading as she desperately racked her brains for something to say to him, something that he would understand. 'It's to do with my career—I've been offered a much better job,' she finally blurted out in despair.

There was another long silence. 'So you've been out with a man who's going to offer you a better job,' he growled angrily. 'Is that what turns you on, Heather? Sleeping with the boss?'

'You've no right to speak to me like that, Ryan—no damn right at all.' Tears were flowing freely now, although her voice stayed remarkably steady.

'Perhaps I didn't make myself clear when I told you that you could stay on in the apartment, honey,' he drawled, his voice laced with ice. 'You stay there because you belong to me and that gives me the right to tell you I don't want you to carry on like some damn call girl.'

'You just want me to be your damn call girl!' she shot back. 'Here in case you should fancy coming home for a few days.'

'If that's how you like to think of it,' Ryan answered coldly.

'Well, you can go to hell!' Before she could even think about what she was doing, she had slammed the phone down, her whole body trembling. As soon as she had done it she regretted it, and snatched up the receiver to ring him back. Only then did she realise that she had no idea where he was staying, and no number for him.

She stared at the receiver in misery. Why had they said those awful things to each other? Why hadn't she told him that she loved him and was missing him? She went to lie down on her bed and waited for him to phone her back, but she waited in vain.

Four days later she moved out of the apartment and checked into a hotel. It was the only thing left to do. She couldn't bear sitting waiting for the phone to ring, and besides, what was the point? Her relationship with Ryan was over. She had known that when she'd discovered she was pregnant. She left most of her possessions behind her as she wasn't well enough to start packing everything up, and she left Ryan a note. Writing that note was the hardest thing of all. It was cold and stilted, as if she were writing it to a stranger, not the man who was the father of her child, the person she loved more than anyone in the world.

The pains in her stomach started again not long after she moved into the hotel. It was like a nightmare. She was terrified to get out of bed in case she lost the baby and there was no one there for her. She had never felt so alone. She couldn't even ring the few friends she had made at work because when she had phoned to tell them she wouldn't be back she had told them she had a new job and was moving away.

When her doctor came he lost no time in having her admitted to hospital. And that was where she spent the rest of her pregnancy. It was quite a relief to get into that hospital bed—at least she felt safe in there and her baby would have a better chance. But the time dragged heavily, her mind dwelling on Ryan. She wondered if he ever thought about her, if he missed her. Then one day her questions were unexpectedly answered.

She was leafing through a glossy magazine when her attention was arrested by the picture of a beautiful woman. She had hair like golden silk, skin that glowed with vitality, and a body that was sensuously perfect. Above her the caption read "Annabel Rothstar. Twenty-two, and one of America's richest women."

Quickly Heather read on, realising that this was the women whom Ryan had been conducting business with. She skipped over the blurb about Annabel's being an up-and-coming young actress until she reached what she had been searching for. "Annabel had no serious affairs until recently, when she has been seeing a lot of industrialist Ryan Jameson."

So much for Ryan's missing her, she thought with black despair. She tried desperately not to get upset—that was the worst thing she could do for her baby. But it was hard when all she wanted to do was cry and cry. . .

Heather stared at the rows of clothes facing her, that picture of Annabel Rothstar to the forefront of her mind. Perhaps she should have given in to the temptation of buying a new dress, she thought wearily. Perhaps it would have given her the confidence she needed to get through this weekend. She got up from the bed with a sigh. It would take more than a new dress to help her through the ordeal ahead.

CHAPTER FOUR

HEATHER'S nerves started to flutter every time a car so much as slowed down outside. She glanced at her watch. Ryan's arrival was imminent; he had always been punctual when he had picked her up in the past.

'You're not reading the story right,' Sarah suddenly complained from her bed. 'The big bad wolf goes to the pig with the straw house first.'

'So he does.' Heather smiled, flicking back over the page that she had skipped. 'I don't think you need me to read this story. You know it off by heart.' Her eyes wandered towards the window again.

A car was slowly pulling up outside and she stood up quickly as she saw Ryan's tall figure climbing out. 'Here he is now,' she muttered, going towards the door to call Susan.

'Who, the big bad wolf?' Sarah asked, her eyes wide and blue in her small face.

'No, darling.' Heather gave a wry smile at what could be a very accurate description of Ryan Jameson. Just as long as her house wasn't made out of straw! she thought, with a tinge of almost hysterical humour. 'I have to go now, darling, but Susan will finish the story for you,' she said as she moved to hug the little girl. She put a hand on Sarah's forehead before she stood up—it was still very hot. Reluctantly she turned towards the door as Susan came in. 'I'll ring you tonight and give you my number just in case,' she told her.

She had to swallow down a lump in her throat as she

glanced back at the tiny figure of her daughter. She was still only a baby and Heather felt so incredibly guilty about leaving her. Her eyes misted with tears as she picked up her bag and coat from beside the door, where she had left them for a speedy exit. She didn't dare glance back again as she closed the bedroom door and crossed the hall. If she had done, she would probably have broken down. She was anxious to get out of her apartment as quickly as possible because she didn't want to give Ryan a chance to set foot inside it. She practically ran through the front door and collided straight into Ryan's broad frame.

His arms moved immediately around her waist to steady her, and for a breathless second she was held close in a familiarly warm embrace that made her heart thud helplessly.

'Sorry.' She wrenched herself away from him after a few disorientated moments and tried to blink away the tears in her dark eyes as she looked up at his formidably handsome face.

He frowned, a strange expression in his deep blue eyes as they moved over her neat figure in the cream and cinnamon suit and then lingered on the paleness of her face and her shimmering eyes. She knew that sharp gaze was well aware of the tears glimmering there and she looked hurriedly away.

'Are you ready to go?' he asked coldly as he reached to take her case.

She nodded and turned to close the door behind her.

'You've left your television on,' Ryan observed in a dry tone, his blue eyes never leaving her face.

Heat rose up under her delicate porcelain skin as she realised that Susan had left the appliance turned on and the noise from it was drifting clearly out towards them.

She hesitated nervously, unsure of what to do. If she returned into the apartment she would run the risk of Ryan following her and that was far too dangerous. There might be some of Sarah's toys lying around, or, worse still, the little girl might hear them and come running out. No, she couldn't chance going back in.

She lifted her head in an unconsciously defiant manner. 'I've left someone to look after the apartment.'

'I see.' Ryan's voice was filled with scathing contempt and he turned abruptly to go down the stairs towards the street.

What on earth was the matter with him? Heather wondered, following his brisk steps.

It was bitterly cold outside and it was a relief to climb into the comfortable warmth of Ryan's silver Lamborghini. He started the powerful engine as she fastened her seatbelt. There was a strained silence which neither made any attempt to break as Ryan pulled the car into the busy stream of traffic.

Heather couldn't help glancing back and up towards Sarah's lighted window. She hoped her daughter was going to be all right while she was away. What if her temperature increased and she started to cry for her during the night? Heather swallowed, trying desperately to contain the tears that lodged like a tight knot in her throat.

'For God's sake, Heather, you're only leaving him for one night.' Ryan's voice cut harshly into her thoughts and she turned startled eyes on him. He thought that she had a man in her apartment—realisation dawned suddenly! And by the look of disdain on his face he probably thought it was Richard Craven. The idea was so ludicrous that she had to smile.

'Are you living with him?' The abrupt question

wiped the smile clean away.

'I don't think my personal life is any of your business,' she answered icily, turning to glare out at the dark Manchester streets.

The silence seemed to stretch forever as Ryan manoeuvred the car through the busy Friday evening traffic. Heather couldn't help but admire the competent way he handled the powerful car. He had always been a good driver, she remembered. She had always felt safe with him. Her hands clenched into tight fists and she slid a sideways glance at him.

He looked more relaxed now, not as angry as before, although a frown still hovered slightly over the broad forehead. Her eyes moved down over the straight nose to the firm line of his lips and then to the cleft in his strong jaw. If it was possible, he seemed to have grown even more handsome over the last few years. He would be thirty-five now, and his hair still had that dark, rich quality. His skin was tanned with the healthy glow of the outdoors, making her wonder how long he had been back from the States.

'Have I changed much over the last few years?' he enquired suddenly, without taking his eyes from the road.

She flushed and glanced down at her hands, embarrassed that he had noticed her scrutiny. 'Not much,' she muttered almost inaudibly.

'You have.' His eyes moved from the road to flicker over her slim figure briefly. 'You look different somehow.'

I suppose I do, she thought grimly. Giving birth to his child hadn't exactly left her untouched. There were subtle changes in her body and she was no longer the carefree girl she had been when she first met Ryan.

'You said you husband died a few years ago,' he remarked casually, returning his attention to the road. 'You couldn't have been married very long. It's what . . . nearly four and a half years since our affair ended.'

For some reason the casual way he referred to their relationship in that way hurt her. She couldn't for the life of her fathom out why it should do so—after all, their association in the past could only be described as an affair. That was all it had been, a brief interlude that meant very little to Ryan. The fact that it had changed her whole way of life was irrelevant, she thought with uncharacteristic bitterness. Not that she had any regrets about Sarah—she was the only thing that made Heather's life seem worthwhile.

'Then about six months later you married Edwards,' Ryan went on drily. 'Didn't wait long, did you, Heather?'

She shot a startled glance at the remote harshness of Ryan's face. Six months! That was the time she had decided to change her name and make a whole new life for herself. How on earth had he pin-pointed the time of her supposed marriage so accurately?

'Lyn Perry informed me of the union when I was home on business soon after.' He answered the unspoken question, turning cold blue eyes down on her. 'She told me that she had bumped into you outside some shop and that you were glowing with happiness.'

Lyn Perry, of course! Heather turned away from that disconcerting blue gaze. She remembered that meeting with Lyn very vividly. She had hardly been able to believe her misfortune in bumping into a woman who had been the most malicious gossip of the Harper's office. Her one consolation had been that at least she hadn't had Sarah with her in her pram—that would have been a nightmare.

Lyn had lost no time of course in informing Heather of how well Mr Jameson was doing in America, dating a very beautiful heiress. She had prattled on for a full fifteen minutes about it, interspersed with comments along the lines of, "What a pity things didn't work out for you, dear," until Heather had felt like screaming. When Lyn had finally taken breath to ask her what she was doing now, Heather had only got a small measure of satisfaction in telling her she was shopping for her wedding trousseau for next week before walking quickly away. The episode had left her feeling sick and uneasy; she certainly hadn't been glowing with happiness. It was just after that when she had decided to move away from London and had changed her name. She hadn't wanted to run even the slightest risk of running into anyone she knew again. Next time she might not be so lucky—she might have Sarah with her, and the thought that someone would look at her baby and guess the truth made her blood run cold.

'She didn't seem to know who the mystery man was, only that you were very happy and he was very wealthy,' Ryan went on, his voice heavy with mockery. 'I presume he was your new boss?'

Heather stared straight ahead as the powerful headlights of the Lamborghini sliced through the dense blackness of the country roads they were now travelling over. She might have guessed that Lyn would add her own embellishments to what she thought was a juicy piece of gossip. 'You presume far too much,' she told him in a stiff, angry voice. 'And for your information my husband was not a wealthy man.'

'Miscalculated, did you, Heather?' he said with grim

amusement. 'That's really too bad. Maybe you will have better luck with Richard Craven.'

'And what the hell is that supposed to mean?' she rounded on him furiously.

'Oh, come now, Heather, there's no need to be coy with me. You're forgetting that I know you very well. I know that behind that beautiful feminine body there is a very cold and calculating woman. I'm sure it hasn't escaped your notice that Robert Craven is pushing sixty and will no doubt be handing his company on to his son very soon. Although I'm sure that has nothing to do with the fact that you're now sleeping with the guy,' he finished on a heavy note of sarcasm.

Heather's breath escaped in an outraged gasp. 'That is just about the most disgusting thing I have ever heard. God, you really are a hateful man!' She practically spat the words at him.

One dark eyebrow rose in droll amusement. 'That wasn't the way you used to describe me in the past, Heather. Whatever happened to the tender endearments, the passionate kisses? They seemed to die a pretty quick death when you thought you'd found yourself a better catch.'

'Yes, well, that seems to have cut both ways, doesn't it, Ryan? Don't try to tell me that you waited more than a couple of days when you got to the States before you filled the space in your bed,' she flung back angrily.

'I'm not going to try and tell you anything,' he answered drily, then shot her a hard glance. 'Was that your roundabout way of asking me about my love-life?'

'Certainly not!' She gave a small laugh which sounded unnatural in the heavy silence of the moment. 'I have no doubt that your sex life has been as active as ever, and I wouldn't dream of asking you about love, as

I'm sure you don't even understand the meaning of that word. The only thing you have ever been able to comprehend is control and possession,' she lashed out, heedless of the dark, ominous expression on his face and the way his mouth had tightened into a thin, cruel line. It was only as the car started to slow down and he pulled it to a standstill in a dark lay-by that she realised just how incautious she had allowed her tongue to be.

'How come you seem to be such an expert on the word love all of a sudden?' Ryan derided in a low, rasping tone. 'What wonderful man managed to introduce these finer feelings to you?'

For a moment Heather felt real fear. His anger seemed to be washing over her in tangible waves, making her aware of the close confines of the car and the velvet black of night that shrouded the remote country lane.

'I never professed to being an expert, Ryan,' she managed to say calmly. 'But I think I have learnt a little since our time together.'

'From Edwards or Craven?' He turned completely in his seat to glare down at her with cutting blue eyes. When she made no attempt to answer him his lips twisted scornfully. 'And are you going to inform me exactly what it was you learnt?'

'Look, Ryan, I——'

'Or maybe, if you're reluctant to tell me in words, I should try to discover that answer another way,' he cut across her stumbling voice abruptly, moving closer towards her body, a strange expression on his handsome features.

'Ryan!' She recoiled instantly, his name a horrified gasp in the silence.

His eyes moved to where one slender hand had

instinctively reached towards the door-handle, and a grim smile tugged at his lips. 'Why, Heather, I do believe you are frightened of me,' he remarked in a silky tone. 'What did you think I was going to do—kiss you?' He watched the hot colour scorch her skin with cool dispassion. 'Sorry to disappoint you, honey, but I wasn't after your lips or your body.' He stretched across her and opened the glove compartment to take out a small remote-control box. 'Only this,' he said, pointing it towards large wrought-iron gates to one side of them so that they swung open.

The red-hot heat of embarrassment continued to eat away at Heather as he drove the car up through the long, winding driveway of what was obviously his country estate. She had thought he was going to kiss her. For one heart-stopping moment she had felt sure that his lips were coming down towards hers, and the awareness that thought had stirred up inside her had been electric. She clenched her hands into tight fists, her nails digging into the tender skin of her palms as she strove desperately to get her emotions under tight control.

Ryan flicked a glance towards her. 'Of course, if you're all that anxious to show me what you've learnt over the last four and a half years we can always arrange something for later on tonight.' he murmured drily.

'Go to hell, Ryan,' she muttered furiously, realising that he was deliberately taunting her, enjoying her agitation. 'If you were the last man in the world I wouldn't want you anywhere near me.'

'Now that I find hard to believe,' he grated harshly. 'You may have rocks where your heart should be, but you body always responded very passionately to me.'

Once again mortifying heat seared through her as his words conjured up pictures she would rather not remember. 'I was also a very good actress,' she assured him through clenched teeth.

He gave a low rumble of laughter. 'If that was acting, honey, you deserve an Academy award.'

'This is not a subject I care to discuss, Ryan,' she said sharply. 'I have come here to discuss business and if you were any kind of a gentleman you wouldn't——'

'Wouldn't what? Refer to the fact that we were once lovers?' he cut in abruptly. 'Or are you more frightened that I might try to prove that the one thing that was real between us was the passion?'

'Don't be ridiculous,' she told him in a small, shaky voice. She watched as the car rounded a bend and a large house loomed in front of them. It looked more like a stately home than a private residence. Its leaded windows were ablaze with bright golden light that spilled out into the darkness of the night, lighting up the courtyard in front of it where Ryan brought the Lamborghini to an abrupt halt.

'Am I?' He turned to smile at her coolly. 'Well, one thing is for sure—I never laid any claims to being a gentleman.'

She watched the downward descent of his head with a strange sensation of shock and disbelief. She would scream if he dared to touch her. She abhorred him coming anywhere near her. She would lash out at him if he so much as . . .

His face closed out the light from the house. He was so close that she could feel the whisper of his breath against her skin. It sent prickles of awareness shooting through her and her mind whirled into confusion. Then his lips moved down on to hers, gently at first as they explored their trembling softness. Heat seemed to ignite inside her and there was a strange feeling in the pit of her stomach as if she were on some sort of roller-coaster that had overshot its rails and was plunging with the speed of light down a deep, endless chasm.

'Ryan?' Was that low, husky groan really coming from her? He pushed her further back into her seat and his hand moved caressingly up over the curve of her hip and waist before moving to cover the soft swell of her breast. Her body seemed to come to life under his touch, and she shuddered with pleasure as his thumb rubbed over the hardening peak of her breast. Her lips responded to his now with a deep, urgent need, all caution and fear forgotten in his arms, then, totally unexpectedly, he had moved away from her. She blinked in dazed confusion, her body feeling strangely cold after the heat of his caress.

'How much of that was an act, Heather?' he enquired in a dry, uneven voice. 'Or don't you know?'

She stared at him, mesmerised by the dense blueness of his eyes, held like a startled moth in the full beam of powerful lights. She shook her head helplessly, unable to find her voice or her thoughts.

'I don't suppose you even know the answer to that,' he grated harshly. 'You've probably played your games for so long now that you don't know what's real and what's feigned any more.'

A brooding bitterness darkened her eyes. 'I think you've made your point, Ryan,' she murmured quietly.

'Do you?' His mouth compressed as he turned to open the door of the car. 'I don't think I've even begun to make my point.' Bitter coldness swept into the car as he climbed out, and she hugged slender arms around her body. She was shivering convulsively, but it wasn't from the cold; it was more a reaction to the way Ryan had kissed her, the way she had responded so easily. He had merely been establishing the fact that he had held a certain power over her senses at one time and still did. Her avowal to the contrary had obviously piqued his male pride. She was appalled by just how easily he had proved his point; it made her face burn and her mind writhe in humiliated anguish. At this moment she hated Ryan more than she ever had before.

With a sigh she forced herself to push open the car door and walk around to where he was unloading their bags from the boot. His eyes raked over her contemptuously and for the first time Heather recognised dislike in that blue gaze, a dislike that almost seemed to outweigh her own for him.

For some reason the realisation made her heart squeeze painfully. She should hardly be surprised at Ryan's animosity towards her. After all, he had once regarded her as his possession and she had left him before he had dismissed her properly. Left him and, to all intents and purposes, married another man. A man like Ryan Jameson would never let his vanity forget such a thing.

They walked up the smooth white marble steps towards the impressive front door in terse silence.

It was beautifully warm inside, which surprised Heather as the house was extremely vast. The entrance itself was as large as a ballroom, a magnificent staircase sweeping down into its centre. The fresh scent of tangy pine hung in the air and Heather guessed it must have come from the enormous Christmas tree that shimmered in brilliant glory at the base of the stairway.

A plump woman with a good-natured, smiling face had just bent to sweep up a few offending pine needles that had dared to fall on to the thick, luxurious red carpet, but as they stepped in she left her task at once to hurry towards them. 'It's good to have you home again, Mr. Jameson,' she said, and then smiled brightly at Heather.

'Thank you, Mrs Marton. This is Heather Edwards, who will be staying until Sunday when she will return to Manchester with me.' Ryan passed Heather's light holdall towards his housekeeper. 'Have you prepared the garden suite for her as I asked?'

'I have, sir.' Mrs Marton smiled. 'Miss Rothstar and Mr Michaels have already arrived; they are in the drawing-room.'

'Ah, good.' Ryan put a guiding hand on Heather's arm. 'We'll go in, then.'

For some reason Heather felt incredibly nervous as Ryan opened the panelled double doors into the drawing-room. What was the matter with her? she wondered bleakly. Surely she wasn't bothered about meeting Ryan's girlfriend?

A log fire burned brightly in a massive stone fireplace and two people rose from the deep blue velvet settees on either side of it as they entered the room.

'There you are, honey!' Annabel Rothstar moved gracefully across the room. She was tall and elegant, dressed in the latest of designer suits which showed every curve of her beautiful body to perfection. She was simply the most stunning woman Heather had ever seen. Certainly those glossy pictures she had once looked at when she lay in her hospital bed hadn't done the woman justice, and those she had thought were disturbingly perfect.

She pouted deep rose-pink lips and reached up to kiss Ryan's cheek. 'We were beginning to think you'd got lost,' she murmured in a soft American accent.

'Dreadful bad manners to be late for one's guests.'

Ryan grinned ruefully. 'But I'm sure you and Simon welcomed the rest after your long flight.' Ryan turned slightly towards Heather. 'Let me introduce you to Heather Edwards,' he said smoothly. Heather noticed how his hand lingered lightly at the other woman's tiny waist. 'Heather, this is Annabel Rothstar and her cousin Simon Michaels. They flew in from California today.'

Heather smiled politely and wondered how anyone could look so good after a long transatlantic flight.

Simon Michaels came forward and clasped her hand warmly. 'Well, now, this is a lovely surprise.' He grinned, his blue eyes moving over her with an appreciative gleam. He was a good-looking man. Heather judged him to be about twenty-five or -six—about the same age as Annabel. There was a similarity to the beautiful woman at his side in the well-defined cheekbones and the golden-blond hair. They were the type of couple you would expect to find on the cover of an illustrious magazine.

'Pay no attention to him, Heather,' Annabel inserted in a dry tone. 'He's a born womaniser, just can't help himself.'

Simon's eyebrows rose and he turned a disdainful eye on the other woman. 'When Heather is in need of a guardian angel I'm sure she will hire you, cousin dear,' drawled in a sarcastic tone. The atmosphere between the two of them seemed to crackle with tension, making Heather wonder if they had been arguing before she and Ryan came in.

'Are you two bickering again?' Ryan enquired with dry humour as he crossed towards the drinks cabinet.

'Of course not, we never argue,' Simon answered, with such a look of amusement in his blue eyes that Heather judged that to be the understatement of the year.

He sat back into the deep settee and patted the space next to him for Heather to sit down.

'These two are like cat and dog,' Ryan told Heather as he passed her a crystal glass of sparkling wine. 'As a matter of principle they never agree on anything.'

'That's not true, darling.' Annabel sat down on the settee opposite and her blue eyes were cold as they glared at Simon. 'We both agree that working together was the worst mistake of our lives.'

'What are you working on?' Heather asked, sipping her wine and watching as Ryan settled himself close to Annabel on the settee.

'We've got starring roles opposite each other in a new film that's being made for television. It's a real breakthrough into the big time for my acting career.'

'And it's the end of mine,' Simon muttered under his breath.

'What was that, Simon dear?' Annabel enquired in an icy tone.

'You heard,' he growled angrily.

'Well, now, isn't this cosy?' Ryan drawled in deep amusement.

'Oh, Ryan, I am sorry!' Annabel rested her blonde head against his broad shoulders. 'It's awful of us to behave like this when you have been good enough to throw this party for the film crew this evening, and you're allowing us to film some location shots here. I don't know how I'll ever thank you, you're absolutely wonderful.'

She reached up to kiss his cheek and he grinned down at her. 'I'm sure I'll think of something.'

Heather felt her heart squeeze painfully as she watched them. They looked so right together and they obviously adored each other. She took a sip of her wine and it seemed to stick in an uncomfortable knot in her throat. She swallowed determinedly. What was the matter with her? She didn't give a damn who Ryan was in love with; she wasn't interested in anything to do with him.

Simon finished his drink and put the glass down on the table with a sharp thud. 'Well, I think I'll go on up to my room and get ready for tonight's festivities,' he murmured.

'Good idea.' Annabel straightened and got gracefully to her feet, running a smoothing hand over her long blonde hair. 'We'll see you later, then.' She gave a brilliant smile at both Ryan and Heather and then, after she linked her hand through Simon's arm, they left the room as if they were the best of friends.

'Pay no attention to Annabel's firework displays.' Ryan grinned at Heather. 'It's her artistic temperament.'

'No doubt.' Heather couldn't keep the acerbity from her voice.

'What do you think of her for the advertisement now that you've seen her?' he went on smoothly.

Heather shrugged. 'As you said, she certainly captures the attention. But will she have time to do an ad, considering she is in the middle of doing a film?'

'She'll be around this area for a while now, so I think I'll be able to persuade her,' Ryan answered confidently. 'We'll discuss it with her tomorrow when she gets up, which, knowing Annabel, will probably be around midday.' He grinned.

'Well, you would know,' Heather couldn't help herself retorting sharply.

There was a knock at the door and Mrs Marton came in, interrupting whatever would have been his reply. 'Some more of your guests have arrived, Mr Jameson.

Shall I show them to their rooms?'

Ryan nodded. 'Yes, I'll just come out and have a word first.' He rose with lithe ease to his feet. 'I won't be long, Heather,' he murmured.

Heather sat quietly gazing into the fire for a moment after they left, trying to blank out the feelings of tension invading her body. Seeing Ryan and Annabel together had stirred up strange emotions within her—emotions that she had no wish even to acknowledge. Confused, Heather looked away from those bright blazing flames and her eye fell on the telephone sitting on the table to one side of her. She should be thinking about her child, not brooding over things that were best left in the past. Quickly she got to her feet. She would ring home while she had this opportunity.

Susan answered almost immediately. 'Oh, I'm glad you've phoned, Mrs Edwards. I'm having difficulty getting Sarah to sleep. Maybe if you would talk to her it would do the trick.'

Heather bit her lip. 'Other than that, is she all right? How is her temperature?'

'She's still a bit hot, but no worse than she was,' Susan assured her. 'Shall I take your number before I let you talk to her? Then if I need you I'll just phone.'

'Yes . . . yes, of course.' Heather glanced down at the phone and read the number for her, then she waited for her to hand the phone over to Sarah.

'Are you all right, darling?' she asked anxiously. 'Are you being a good girl for Susan?'

'Yes,' came the small, tremulous reply. 'When are you coming home, Mumma?'

'I told you, darling, I'll be home on Sunday ready to read you a bedtime story.'

'Promise?' The small voice quivered slightly.

'Yes, I promise,' Heather assured her firmly. 'Will you be a good girl and go to sleep for Susan now?'

'I suppose,' came the reluctant reply.

Heather smiled. 'All right, sweetheart, I'll see you on Sunday.' Heather vaguely heard a soft click behind her, but all her attention was tuned in on her daughter. 'Love you too,' she said softly as she replaced the receiver.

'How touching.' Ryan's deep voice behind her made her jump, and she swung around, her heart thudding nervously, her eyes wide in the pallor of her face. Just how much of her conversation had he heard? she wondered frantically.

'Sounds as though you've successfully hooked another big fish,' Ryan went on in a jeering tone. 'When are you planning on reeling him in for the kill?'

'I don't know what you're talking about.' She frowned.

'I'm talking about Craven.' He jerked his head towards the phone in a disparaging manner. 'I bet the poor fool didn't know what had hit him when you turned those beautiful scheming eyes in his direction.'

Although his words stirred up anger inside her, there was also an overwhelming sense of relief—if Ryan thought she had been speaking to a man he couldn't have heard much of her conversation. 'That was a private call, Ryan, and none of your business. I will of course pay you for it, if that is what's bothering you.'

His lips curved in a disdainful, jeering smile. 'That's always the bottom line with you, isn't it, Heather? Money.'

Suddenly Heather's temper snapped. She was tired of his disgusting accusations and it was obvious that, no matter how she denied them, it wasn't going to make a blind bit of difference to him. 'All right, so I love money,' she told him with cool flippancy. 'I adore nice clothes, beautiful jewellery, a good standard of living. Why else do you think I moved in with you?' she blazed.

The words lingered in the stillness of the room. Harsh, bitter words that were utterly unforgivable. As soon as she had said them she wanted to call them back, but that of course was impossible. One look at Ryan's dark, menacing face told her that.

'So now we have the real Heather Edwards,' he grated harshly. 'You want to be careful, my sweet. One day things might rebound in your pretty face, and it will hurt like hell. I just hope I'm somewhere around to see it happen.'

CHAPTER FIVE

HEATHER took her time getting ready for the party that evening. She soaked in a long, luxurious bath in the en-suite bathroom of her room and then, wrapping herself in a large, soft towel, walked through to her bedroom to relax for a while on top of the satin and lace quilt that covered the exquisite four-poster bed.

It was a beautiful room, she thought idly as she glanced around at the pale embossed walls. The décor was superb, the furniture obviously all priceless antiques that fitted in so well with the opulent surroundings.

The whole house was spectacular and full of character. If circumstances had been different she would have thoroughly enjoyed a stay here. As it was, she could hardly wait to get away; the whole thing was a nightmare. She thought about the way she had spoken to Ryan earlier and felt sick again. Goaded beyond endurance, she had found it so easy to lash out like that. It was almost as if Ryan had pushed her towards it, as if he had wanted her to voice all the terrible things he thought about her.

She wondered miserably why his opinion of her was so low. What reasons had she given him for thinking she was cold and calculating? Was it because of all those gifts he had showered on her? She thought about them now—they had mostly been very expensive, beautiful pieces of jewellery. They were the only things that she had made sure to bring with her when she left his apartment and she knew exactly how exorbitantly priced they had been because she had sold them all.

She groaned and turned on her side. She hadn't wanted to sell any of them, they had all held a lot of sentimental value for her, but she had been desperate. She had needed the money to support herself and Sarah when she'd moved north. It had taken time and money to find another apartment and she had been nearly a year out of work before she found a suitable job. She didn't know how she would have survived that year if she hadn't got such a good price for that jewellery. She had been racked with guilt when she'd brought it back to the prestigious shop where Ryan had bought it, but she had salved her conscience by telling herself that the money was his contribution towards his daughter. She shook her head. Ryan couldn't possibly know she had done that. Maybe he was judging her by the note she had left him—that had been a cold, horrible thing to do and he would never know how she had cried copious tears over it, but she had been left with no choice.

She pushed an impatient, trembling hand through long dark hair. What was the point of raking over all this? Ryan's hatred for her probably stemmed from the fact that she had moved out of the apartment before he'd had a chance to throw her out and nothing more.

She glanced at the long blue dress that she had hung up on the outside of her wardrobe. What would this party be like tonight? she wondered nervously. Perhaps she should have bought that new dress; she would look dowdy next to Annabel Rothstar. She was quite sure that the actress would be wearing something very spectacular.

She glanced at her watch and got up to rub some of her favourite Poison body lotion on before slipping into her lace underwear and applying a light make-up. When she finally stepped into her dress, she studied critically her reflection in the long mirror.

The dress was a beautiful colour and that was all that could be said for it. The silky material fell softly over the full curve of her breast, then caught into her tiny waist before flowing down over her slim hips. It emphasised the perfect proportions of her figure, her creamy translucent skin, but Heather didn't notice any of these things—she was far too tense.

Her hair gleamed like a dark raven's wing under the overhead light. It tumbled in silky confusion around her bare shoulders and she hesitated about pinning it up as she had planned. She never wore her hair loose nowadays. Ryan had loved it like this—he had always encouraged her to leave it free and flowing so that he could run his fingers through its silken length. She shook her head to dispel the memory. She would leave it down, but not because of Ryan's preference, only because it suited her better with this dress.

Resolutely she picked up her small evening bag and headed for the door. The sooner she got this evening over, the better she would feel.

She met Simon in the long hallway outside, and was grateful of the fact as she wasn't quite sure how she had been going to find her way back through the maze of corridors towards the stairs. When Mrs Marton had shown her up she had been far too preoccupied with troubled thoughts to note which way they came.

'You look gorgeous,' he said, his blue eyes lighting up in appreciation.

'Thank you,' she smiled. 'You don't look too bad yourself.' In fact he looked very handsome in a midnight-blue suit and white silk shirt that accentuated his tan and his golden hair.

He offered her his arm. 'Can Prince Charming escort you to the ball?' he asked with a grin.

'Certainly.' She smiled, linking arms with him. She laughed as he related an amusing incident about the first time he had played Prince Charming for a children's video. She liked Simon; he wasn't the type that would attract her, but he was extremely amusing and she was thankful for the diversion to take her mind off everything else.

Ryan and Annabel were standing at the bottom of the staircase as they came down, their bodies close together as they spoke in low voices. They looked up as they heard Simon's deep laugh and Heather was glad that she had his arm to lean on as she met Ryan's eyes.

They swept over her, taking in every detail of her appearance with a narrow look that was both cynical and mocking. She couldn't help the flush that stained her delicate skin at that glance. She lifted her chin a little higher and a defiant light entered her dark eyes. How dared he look at her like that? How dared he even presume to judge her?

Her gaze moved towards his companion. She looked stunning in an off-the-shoulder evening gown in a beautiful shade of primrose-yellow. Her blonde hair was loose and gleaming like gold. She looked just like a china doll, fragile, beautiful and very feminine. She was the perfect foil for Ryan's dark, handsome looks that were so overwhelmingly masculine.

'What are you two laughing at?' Annabel asked, looking upwards with a smile.

Simon tapped his nose. 'It was a private joke,' he told her bluntly, making Heather frown. There had been nothing intimate about their conversation; he was just being unnecessarily rude.

'I see.' Annabel didn't let her smile slip; she obviously wasn't too bothered by Simon's manner. Her eyes moved towards Heather. 'You look lovely,' she said brightly. 'That's a very pretty dress—is it by anyone I would know?'

'I doubt it,' Heather answered drily. Annabel would only wear the most expensive of designer labels. She had clearly priced Heather's dress with one disdainful glance.

'Are you sure?' Annabel frowned. 'It looks very familiar. I'm sure one of my college friends had one just like it a few years ago.'

Heather managed to keep her face impassive at that statement. Annabel was either an expert at bitchy remarks or just the most thoughtless person out. Not only had she made it plain that her dress was cheap rubbish, but also that it was not the most fashionable of items. 'You must have a very good memory for trivial details.' she returned lightly.

'I wish you could remember your lines so well——' Simon inserted under his breath.

'You look very beautiful, Heather.' Ryan's deep voice interrupted suddenly, making Heather swing startled eyes towards him.

For a moment their eyes locked and Heather imagined she saw a gleam of tenderness in the sparkling blue depths which aroused the most curious sensation in the pit of her stomach. Then he looked away, his face shuttered, devoid of any emotion, and she knew that she had indeed imagined it.

'Shall we go through and join our guests?' Ryan suggested in a cold, bleak tone.

'Good idea.' Simon grinned at Annabel. 'What do

you say we call a truce tonight, Anna, and go have a dance?'

'Maybe later,' Annabel replied coolly. 'I've promised Ryan the first dance.'

'I see.' Simon's lips compressed tightly as the four of them went down the passageway where the muted sounds of music and laughter drifted down towards them.

The full force of up-tempo music hit them as Ryan opened the large doors into an impressively sized ballroom full of people. Subdued lighting from crystal chandeliers caught the glitter of sequins and diamonds among the crowd. The coffered, mirrored ceiling reflected the sparkle of guests dancing on the polished dance-floor and the sumptuous buffet laid out on a long banqueting table.

Heather hardly had time to take it all in before Simon had caught hold of her arm and started to introduce her to a few people as they made their way through the crowd.

He took two crystal champagne glasses from the tray of a passing waiter and handed her one. 'Cheers.' Simon touched his glass to hers and smiled, but there was an unusual note in his voice and an almost sad look in his blue eyes as he glanced around.

Annabel and Ryan were deep in conversation with some people across the room. Just how serious was their relationship? Heather wondered as she watched them. They seemed very close and obviously Annabel was acting as his hostess for this party. Why hadn't Ryan married her yet? Four and a half years was a long time for him to be seriously involved. Maybe he had been too busy building up his empire to make any commitments. After all, that was what he had told her before he left for the States—he had stated quite categorically that he wasn't ready for marriage. Of course, he would have said that to her as he hadn't been serious about their relationship, but with Annabel things were obviously different.

She turned to find Simon's glance also on the other couple. 'Annabel is very beautiful, isn't she?' Heather remarked, bringing his attention winging back.

'And she knows it,' he replied stiffly.

'I'm surprised someone hasn't snapped her up by now,' Heather continued idly, watching him intently for his reaction.

'She says that she is considering marriage,' Simon said with a biting note in his voice. 'But to be honest I think her first love is her career. She likes to be centre stage in the limelight, and nothing else really matters to her.'

'Sounds as if she has a lot in common with Ryan,' Heather muttered, her hand clenching with alarming force around the slender stem of her champagne glass.

'Why don't we forget about those two and go and have a dance?' Simon suggested with a touch of impatience.

'If you like.'

As they moved around the dance-floor under the glitter of the chandeliers, Heather could see Ryan and Annabel dancing close by. Their bodies were pressed intimately together and Annabel's arms were woven up and around Ryan's broad shoulders. A feeling almost of jealousy pierced through Heather and quickly she tried to shrug it off, feeling impatient with herself. It was no use, the emotion persisted, eating away at her heart like a dull ache.

Maybe it was only natural for her to feel like this, she

thought miserably. Ryan was the father of her child and she had loved him once with all her heart. She shouldn't be too hard on herself for feeling a certain amount of sadness and resentment at seeing him with another woman in his arms.

Simon had said Annabel was considering marriage. Did that mean Ryan had already asked her? She looked over towards the other couple again. Annabel was speaking to him and he was bending his head close, his eyebrows drawn together as he concentrated on her voice. Sarah sometimes looked like that when she was deep in concentration. She was very like her father, the same fiery mahogany lights in her dark hair and those eloquent, vivid blue eyes.

Heather's thoughts lacerated her aching heart and her eyes darkened with pain. She wanted to cry, but the agony inside her was too great for that.

Ryan looked directly at her and hurriedly she glanced away. The next moment she felt a tap on her shoulder and Ryan and Annabel were beside them.

'I think it's time we changed partners, don't you?' Ryan enquired smoothly. Then, before anyone had time to reply, he had pulled Heather towards him and into the hard circle of his arms.

'Are you all right?' he murmured, staring down at her with steady blue eyes that she could hardly bear to meet.

'Of course,' she answered lightly, trying to keep her body firmly away from his.

'Are you sure?' He tipped her chin with a gentle hand so that she was forced to look up at him. 'You looked upset just a few moments ago.'

'Is that very surprising after the words we exchanged earlier?' she snapped. Ryan was sometimes far too perceptive, those eyes too sharp.

'It may have escaped your notice, Heather, but this is a party. I've thrown it to give everyone enjoyment and pleasure and that includes you. I think we should put old grievances behind us for at least the next couple of hours.' He drew her closer so that her body was forced into contact with his. 'Relax,' he murmured softly against her hair.

How could she possibly relax when he was holding her like this? Her heart thudded violently and she closed her eyes, trying to shut out the tender memories that floated into her mind. Memories of Ryan holding her just like this in possessive, strong arms. His dark head bent towards hers so that she could feel his breath against the sensitive skin of her neck and her ear as he whispered soft words to her. Her face flamed with bright scarlet colour as she remembered exactly what he used to say.

The husky sound of Ryan's voice sent *frissons* of electric shivers running through her. 'I always did like your hair like this.' His hand trailed through its silky length, pulling at it gently to tip her head back, exposing the vulnerable creamy face to his intense scrutiny.

She kept her eyes closed, long sooty lashes shutting out his dark features and the inviting curve of his lips.

'Heather . . .' There was a hungry urgency in Ryan's deep voice that evoked an immediate response from her body, a compelling need to be closer to him. She wound her arms up and around his neck so that her breasts were pressed closed against his chest.

'Mmm, that's better.' His soft voice cut through the haze of unreality that surrounded her and suddenly she was remembering how he had held her like this at the airport before walking out of her life.

She jerked away from him, her face ashen-white, her

eyes wide and horrified. What was she doing? Had she completely lost her mind?

With a startled little cry she tore herself from his arms and turned to blindly leave the dance-floor.

Ryan made no move to detain her or go after her, he just watched her pushing her way through the crowd with deep, unfathomable eyes.

'Hey!' Simon caught her arm. 'You look as if there should be steam coming out of your ears.' He grinned. 'In fact, you look just how I feel.'

Despite herself, Heather smiled back at him, the tension receding slightly as she stood next to him. 'Not another argument with Annabel?' she asked lightly.

He nodded and took a long swallow from his glass. 'She's completely impossible these days.' He put his empty glass down and reached for another. 'Care to join me?' he enquired.

She shook her head. 'I think I've had enough for one night. I was just on my way up to my room.'

'So early!' One blond eyebrow rose with disdain.

'Afraid so, I'm feeling tired.' With a rueful smile she bade him goodnight and headed out towards the door.

It seemed even more crowded in the ballroom now, and even though it was heading towards eleven there were still people arriving. It was a struggle to get out into the hall.

Out of the corner of her eye she saw Annabel heading towards her and she tried to summon a smile for the girl as they passed.

Her smile, hesitant as it was, met with such a cold, stony glare that Heather stopped in her tracks. 'Is there something wrong?' she asked with a frown.

'You could say that.' The other woman's voice was low and bitterly angry. 'Just a word of warning,

Heather—keep away from my fiancé. He is in love with me, so unless you are out for a casual fling I'd steer well clear.'

Before Heather had a chance to say anything, the woman moved on, leaving Heather staring after her in perplexity. What on earth had brought that on? Had Annabel resented her dancing with Ryan? Perhaps she knew about their past relationship and felt threatened by it. Well, one thing was certain, Annabel was worrying unnecessarily. Ryan had never had any deep feelings for her and never would.

Heather turned and headed out and up the stairs. She sighed with relief as she closed her bedroom door, and for a moment she leaned back against it, closing her eyes and trying to gain control of her thoughts.

Why had she felt those treacherous responses in her body when Ryan had held her? It had been the same when he had kissed her—she had just melted instantly as if her body was crying out for his every touch. What chemistry occurred when they were together? Why was Ryan able to arouse this yearning need inside her when all other men left her cold?

She shook her head, trying to dismiss the disturbing train of her thoughts, and moved towards the bed. She had a whole day of Ryan's company to get through tomorrow and it wouldn't help matters by thinking like this. She would probably have a whole day of Annabel's company as well because, judging by that woman's face, she didn't think she would be letting Ryan out of her sight tomorrow.

She remembered how Annabel had referred to Ryan as her fiancé—did that mean that they had definite plans to marry? She wasn't wearing an engagement ring, but then maybe Ryan would be remedying that very soon.

The cold feeling that gave her made her seethe with silent fury. So what if they were in love and going to marry? She didn't care one damn. She snatched angrily at the zip fastener at the back of her dress, tearing it down without any thought for the fragile material. Consequently it caught halfway down, lodging into the silky fabric and refusing to budge, no matter how violently she tugged at it.

'Damn!' Her voice was loud and clear in the silence of the room. Now she could neither pull the dress over her head or down past her hips. Frantically she tried to tug the zip back up, but that only seemed to make it worse.

'Heather?' Ryan's voice outside her door made her freeze. 'Heather, are you all right?'

'Of course I'm all right,' she snapped, her voice sounding strangely breathless. 'What do you want?'

'I want to know why you've left the party so early. Are you ill?' he asked patiently.

'No, now go away.' She watched the door nervously, wishing there were some key or bolt that would make her feel less intimidated by his presence. What was he doing up here? She couldn't believe he was in any way concerned about her; she was surprised that he had even noticed that she had left the party.

'Can I come in?'

Panic flooded her body at that softly spoken request. 'Certainly not!' Her voice sounded garbled as the words caught in the sudden dryness of her throat. Nevertheless, she knew that he had heard her and it was with a mixture of anger and fear that she watched the door-handle turn and him stride into the room.

'What's the matter with you?' His eyes raked over her stiff body with cool scrutiny.

Despite the fact that her dress was still decently in place at the front of her body and only hung open at the back, she felt hideously embarrassed. The huge bedroom seemed to have shrunk in size and his powerful frame seemed to dominate it, making her overwhelmingly aware of the intimacy of the situation and of how vulnerable she was to him.

'There is nothing the matter.' She took an instinctive step backwards. 'And how dare you intrude into the privacy of my room?'

'Technically speaking, actually, it's my room.' His firm mouth curved into a grin and his eyes moved to some point behind her. 'What's wrong with your dress?'

'Nothing . . .' Heather's voice trailed off as she turned her head sharply to see what he was looking at. She was mortified to find that he was studying her reflection in the mirror behind, and that he had a complete view of her naked back. He would even know now that she wasn't wearing a bra beneath the silky material of the dress. Flustered, she moved quickly to one side, blocking his line of vision. 'The zip is a little stiff, that's all.' Her chin rose defiantly. 'Now will you please get out of my room so that I can get undressed and go to bed?'

'You still haven't told me why you left the party so abruptly.' His blue eyes moved over the heightened colour of her face and the generous curve of her mouth.

'Because I was tired,' she snapped brusquely. 'Anyway, you haven't invited me here to party. You invited me to talk over your plans for the advertising campaign.'

'Did I?' He raked a distracted hand through the thickness of his hair. 'Ever since I picked you up tonight I've been wondering just why I did invite you here. Why the hell I'm having anything to do with you.'

Heather flinched at that. She knew Ryan's opinion of her was low, but that he should even resent having to do business with her hurt her unbearably. 'Ryan, I know you hate me, but——'

'Forget it, Heather,' he cut across her sharply, suddenly looking tired. 'Come here and I'll fix your zip for you and leave you in peace.'

Her heart thudded like crazy at the unexpected demand and she took a hasty step backwards. 'It's all right, I can manage,' she told him uneasily, cursing herself because her voice sounded so prim and awkward.

'You sound like some demure little virgin,' he rasped harshly. 'Don't be ridiculous, come here while I fix your dress.'

She swallowed down the feelings of hurt and anger and just shook her head stubbornly. Why was it that she felt like crying all of a sudden?

'Oh, for God's sake!' He moved briskly towards her, anger written on every line of his body as he pulled her roughly around to deal with the dress. 'The sight of your naked back isn't going to come as a great shock, considering I know every curve, every inch of your naked body.' She closed her eyes, trembling as much from his words as from the touch of his fingers against her skin. 'After all, you did share my bed for nigh on four months, didn't you, my sweet? Even though it was only in body rather than soul.'

He jerked the zip free, but instead of fastening it up he pulled it slowly down to where it plunged under the line of her lace panties. Her dress would have slithered down completely except that his hand held her by the shoulder, trapping the material and her back close against him. She should have brought her arms up to hold her dress and wrench herself away from him, but she couldn't move. Her whole body seemed to be held in a kind of paralysis.

He bent his head and his lips trailed a heated line over the velvet smoothness of her shoulder and up towards her ear. It unleashed such a wealth of fierce emotion that she felt as if her knees were going to give way beneath her. She probably would have crumpled if he hadn't brought his other hand around her slender waist, drawing her in more firmly against the taut strength of his body.

'You know, Heather, I don't think I do hate you. At this moment it's myself I don't much care for,' he murmured thickly against her ear. 'When you walked into my office last week with those wide, innocent, dark eyes and that delectable curvy figure of yours, I wanted to make love to you again right there and then.' His hand moved against the side of her hip, sending tingling, sharp stabs of awareness shooting through her. 'Have you any idea what it does to a man to want a woman like that, when he knows damn well that she's a cold, unfeeling little witch?'

'Ryan.' Her voice was a low moan of denial as she stretched her head back towards him, wanting the touch of his lips against her skin, wanting him to understand her. Yet her body and her mind were almost incoherent with desire. 'I'm not, I——'

He turned her roughly then, into the circle of his arms. Her dress slipped slightly to one side, but it couldn't move very far as she was held so tightly against him. 'Not what? Hard? Cold? What was that note you left for me at the apartment, then, Heather, if it wasn't all those things?' he rasped violently. 'I tried for a long time to understand that, to comprehend why you left with such indecent haste for the arms of another man. You didn't even wait for me to return home so we could talk it out. I could do nothing but face the brutal facts, your touching concern about the rumours circulating about my state of finances, that loving little note you left and, of course, the jewellery that you disposed of.' His mouth twisted in a bitter smile.

'You knew about that?' Her head jerked up, her eyes glimmering with unshed tears.

'It didn't take a genius to work out that you're not exactly the sentimental type.' His eyes cut into her, icy blue with contempt. 'Those pieces were exceptionally beautiful and very unusual. I'd had them specially made and as far as the jeweller was concerned they might as well have had my name printed all over them——'

'Ryan, please.' Her voice was low and filled with pleading. 'I'm not the calculating person that you believe I am—I had my reasons for selling that jewellery.' Her voice started to break with tears and she desperately tried to get it back under control. 'And as for what I said earlier about moving in with you because . . . because of your money . . .' she shook her head despairingly '. . . it was just a lie, I was angry.'

'Well, then, why did you move in with me?' The harshness of his voice, the grim accusing light in his eyes told her very clearly that it didn't matter what she answered, he would always believe the worst of her. It was too late for them, she would never be able to salvage anything from the past—not even his friendship. If her pride had allowed it she could have told him that she had loved him once, but Ryan had never wanted her love and he would certainly receive such an admission with disdainful amusement. So she allowed the silence to stretch between them, knowing that with every second that ticked away the gulf between them was widening, his misjudgement of her deepening.

His lips twisted in a grim smile. 'You should have been this honest years ago. I've never paid to keep a woman in my bed before, but for you I might have made an exception.' His grip on her seemed to have changed somehow. Now the way he was keeping her pinned firmly against him was frightening, as was the snarl of his voice, the glitter of his eyes.

She knew instinctively that he was going to kiss her, and it would be no warm, tender caress but hard and cold and punishing, teaching her exactly what his feelings for her were. She watched the descent of his dark head almost as if it were happening in slow motion, her eyes wide and terrified.

The rough, brutal pressure of his mouth was every bit as cruel and ruthless as she had expected it to be. She started to tremble violently, but even though her fear must have transmitted itself to him it only made his kiss grow more fiercely intense.

Heather had never been kissed like this before. All her senses screamed out against it, yet the only protest she could make was a small whimpering sound beneath the strength of his mouth. Strangely, that small sound she made deep in her throat seemed to have some effect on the control and oppression of Ryan's lips. His kiss started to change, heat and passion seemed to ignite from nowhere, and shockingly she could feel her mouth responding to it. Warmth and desire began building up between them; she could feel it spreading insidiously right the way through her body. Her lips softened invitingly, her arms started to steal their way up over the powerful expanse of his chest towards his shoulders.

Instantly Ryan seemed to freeze and firmly pushed her away from him. There was a deep stain of colour on his high cheekbones and his eyes were dark midnight-blue as they raked over her slim, trembling body. She had wrapped her arms protectively around herself, holding the silky material of her dress in hands that were tightly clenched.

His face seemed to set into an unyielding, impervious mask as his eyes lingered on the softness of her lips, the deathly pallor of her skin and the dark, wide eyes filled with turbulent emotion. 'Forgive me if I don't follow through and make love to you, my darling.' His voice was deep and rasping in the tense silence. 'But I'm afraid I didn't bring my cheque-book with me.'

Heather's pale skin flamed with horrified anger and hurt. 'Get out of here.' She spat the words at him furiously, her whole body throbbing with the force of her emotions.

When the door closed behind him all she wanted to do was curl up and die. She could hardly believe that he had spoken to her like that and held her and kissed her with such brutal passion. Her whole body burnt as she remembered how she had responded to him. Humiliated and sick at heart, she moved to sit on the edge of her bed.

Ryan's admission that she was still able to arouse him physically had come as a shock to her, but the knowledge that he was able to do the same to her with such relative ease was appalling. Even though his kiss had been callous and punishing she had responded. She had wanted him regardless of his animosity and dislike for her—and that was really frightening.

CHAPTER SIX

HEATHER hardly slept at all that night. She got up at seven o'clock, her head aching, her body tense. She stood under the full jet of the shower for ages, hoping that it would help to relax her, but it just seemed to make her feel worse.

With a heavy sigh she dressed in the attractive cream and cinnamon suit that she had worn to travel in yesterday. How on earth was she going to get through the day ahead? How could she look Ryan in the face, let alone sit and discuss business calmly with him and Annabel?

She flicked a brush lightly through her long hair before securing it firmly up in a severe style away from her face. For a moment she studied her reflection in the mirror, putting a tentative gentle finger against the softness of her lips. They still felt slightly swollen from Ryan's kiss, almost as if he had left the imprint of his strong lips against hers. She shivered convulsively and wished with all her soul that she could pack her small case and creep silently out of the house and away from him. But that was the coward's way out, she thought briskly as she applied some light make-up to disguise the ravages from the night before. She would have to face Ryan and deal with the situation.

She passed the phone in the hall at the base of the stairs and wondered if she should ring Susan. She glanced at her watch and decided against it. It was too early yet, and if Susan had had a late night with Sarah she would need a rest this morning.

'Good morning, Ms Edwards.' Mrs Marton glanced around the doorway that led through to the kitchen. 'You're up bright and early. Would you like some breakfast?'

'Just some coffee, please.' Heather smiled wanly. She glanced down the long passageway towards the ballroom. The door was open and the room empty. The banqueting table was polished to a high brilliance and all the debris from the party cleared away.

'Looks as if you were busy tidying up last night,' Heather remarked as she followed the other woman into the large luxurious kitchen.

'Oh, goodness me, no!' Mrs Marton laughed. 'Mr Jameson always hires more staff on these occasions. I went off to bed.' She poured some fresh coffee from a percolator into a china cup. 'Would you like this in the drawing-room or the lounge?' she asked politely.

'I'd sooner just have it in here with you—that is, if I'm not in the way?'

'No, of course not.' The housekeeper hastily set the cream jug and coffee down on to the kitchen table and Heather sat down.

'Why don't you join me?' she invited, and Mrs Marton smiled.

'I might as well—everyone is still in bed. I think the party must have been a success.'

'Yes.' Try as she did, Heather could not raise any enthusiasm for last night's party.

'Mr Jameson's up, of course.' The housekeeper went on. 'He always gets up early and goes out to the stables when he's home. He likes to ride first thing in the morning.'

Heather could feel her nerves coiling into tight knots.

She hoped Ryan wouldn't come in for a while. Despite all the brave counselling she had given herself upstairs, she did not feel ready to face him. 'Have you worked for Ryan long?' She tried to make idle conversation to take her mind off her fears.

'About three years, since Mr. Jameson bought this house. And they have been very happy years too,' Mrs Marton told her forthrightly.

'I take it you get on well with your employer.' Heather smiled and sipped her coffee.

'Oh, he is a wonderful man, generous and good. I worry about him sometimes though—he works far too hard. Hardly ever has a chance to relax at home. He's either in the States or in London on business, and when he does come home here he seems to spend most of the time at his offices in Manchester. He's just a workaholic—what free time he has seems to be filled with charity organisations.' Mrs Marton poured herself a drink and grinned ruefully. 'I have rattled on. You'll have to excuse me, but once I get on the subject of Mr Jameson I can't seem to help myself. He's such a good man. I just hope he's going to settle down one of these days and find himself a nice wife. I'm sure sometimes that he works so hard because he's trying to fill that void in his life.'

He will probably fill that position a lot sooner than you think, Heather thought as she stared down bleakly at the cup in front of her.

The shrill ring of the phone made her nerves jump and she watched anxiously as Mrs Marton picked it up from the kitchen extension.

'It's for you,' she said, turning towards Heather with a frown.

'Me?' Heather stumbled as she got up too quickly. It

could only be Susan, and that must mean that there was something wrong. Her hand was shaking as she took the receiver from the other woman.

'I'm really sorry to bother you so early, Ms Edwards.' Susan's voice sounded distraught. 'But Sarah's had an awful night and her temperature is way up. I was wondering if I should phone for a doctor?'

Heather's heart pounded violently and her mouth felt dry with fear. 'Yes, ring the doctor straight away. You know where his number is in the book beside the phone?'

'Yes, I'll do it now,' Susan assured her.

'Good, and I'm on my way home now.' As she replaced the receiver she turned to look at the house-keeper, who was watching her with a look of concern. 'I've got to go back to Manchester immediately,' she told her urgently.

'Mr Jameson might still be in the stables—if you hurry you just might catch him.' Mrs Marton opened the back door and pointed down towards the end of the courtyard. 'Turn right and hopefully you will find him down there.' The older woman turned anxious eyes on her. 'I hope to God he hasn't gone.'

'So do I.' Heather ran as fast as she could down over the cobble-stones. Thankfully her heels weren't too high, otherwise it would have been impossible to hurry.

It was a sharp, cold morning and an icy mist hung over everything. There was a smell of woodsmoke in the air and a stillness that seemed heavy and somehow menacing.

She turned the corner and saw the stables. A few of the half-doors were open and horses watched her progress down the yard with silent brown eyes.

There was no sign of Ryan and Heather could feel her

stomach clenching with fear as she reached the end of the stalls.

Suddenly there was a clatter of hoofs and Ryan was in front of her, astride a powerful-looking black stallion. Its flanks gleamed in the early morning light and its eyes rolled impatiently as Ryan kept a tight control of the reins.

He looked very much the lord and master seated up there. He was dressed in dark trousers and riding jacket, his blue eyes formidable as they swept over the paleness of her face and the dark hair that was swept back, making her look disturbingly vulnerable.

'What are you doing out here?' he demanded harshly.

'Looking for you.' Her nerves were twisting in distress as she looked up at him. 'I have to go home, Ryan.'

'Really?' His dark brows shot up disdainfully. 'Can't stand to be away from the man you adore for one moment longer, I suppose?' His voice dripped with sarcasm as he glared down at her.

Heather shook her head helplessly. 'No, nothing like that. I just have to go back straight away. I . . . I just have to,' she finished, her voice trembling slightly, her eyes wide and imploring.

'Why?' The sharp question made her nerves quiver and there was fear and uncertainty on her face. For the life of her she couldn't think of one excuse she could give him; she never had been any good at lying.

Because our baby is sick! She wanted to scream the words at him, but of course she couldn't. 'Please, Ryan,' she whispered. 'I just want to go.'

His lips tightened derisively. 'I see,' he answered roughly, and there seemed to be a wealth of meaning that she couldn't understand behind his words. 'Well,

I'm not ready to let you go.' His eyes were a brilliant blue, as cold as the sky on a January day. 'Besides, we haven't discussed our plans for the advertisement yet, and I want us both to talk to Annabel this afternoon.'

'I can't.' Heather's voice rose sharply and the horse moved nervously, its hoofs scraping over the cobbles, its breath flaring like grey smoke in the frosty air. It was a measure of Ryan's expertise as a rider that he was able to keep the highly strung thoroughbred under tight control.

Heather moved back from the animal before continuing. 'Something more important has come up——'

'Nothing is that important,' Ryan cut in, his voice low with contempt. Then he turned the horse towards the rolling countryside that stretched behind him. 'We'll discuss it when I get back.'

'No, Ryan . . . please!' she called out, but it was too late. He had given the black stallion its head, and its long, powerful limbs were reaching out in a fast gallop across the hard, frosty ground.

Tears welled up inside Heather as she watched him go. That was typical of Ryan—he wasn't able to comprehend that anything was more important than business. There was no way he would take her back to the city until he was good and ready. He was the master, and he would decide what was important and what was unworthy of his attention. Her sudden wish to go home had just been dismissed as a mere feminine whim.

She turned back towards the house, her heart heavy, her mind filled with torturing images of Sarah's pale, delicate face against the pillows of her bed, crying for her.

Mrs Marton took one look at Heather's face and

jumped to the wrong conclusion. 'You missed him!' she murmured in dismay.

Heather didn't answer; she felt too upset to even talk about it. 'I don't suppose there's a railway station somewhere near?' she asked, sitting down at the kitchen table, running her hands over her long hair.

'Afraid not, we're rather isolated out here,' Mrs Marton answered. 'Did I hear you say that someone was sick?' she asked suddenly. 'Is that the problem?'

Heather nodded her head absently.

'Are you able to drive?' Mrs Marton asked. 'Because if so, Mr Jameson has an Alfa Romeo sitting in the garage. I'm sure he wouldn't mind you using it because he lets his guests use it sometimes.'

Heather's head jerked up with interest. She knew that Ryan would mind if she took his car—he had already made his feelings clear about her leaving—but right at this moment she didn't care. All she cared about was getting home to Sarah. 'It's been a while since I've been behind the wheel of a car, but I can drive.'

'Right, well, the keys should be over here.' Mrs Marton moved briskly towards one of the kitchen cabinets, opening it up to reveal a large board with row upon row of keys all neatly labelled. 'Now that's strange!' The housekeeper frowned. 'They're not here.'

Heather's heart sank. 'Maybe Ryan put them down somewhere else,' she murmured. 'In his room perhaps?'

'They could be in his office, but it's most unusual for him to put them in there. He's very methodical about these things.' The woman closed the cabinet door and then hesitated. 'I don't know if I should look for them in his office. I don't really like to disturb anything in there.' She glanced across at Heather, catching the anguished expression in her dark eyes and shrugged.

'Well, as it's an emergency, I'm sure Mr Jameson wouldn't mind.'

Not only would Ryan mind, he would be absolutely furious, Heather thought grimly a little while later as she slipped into the gleaming red Alfa which sat in the garage. Her hands trembled slightly as she inserted the key in the ignition and the powerful engine flared into life.

For a moment she sat quietly, trying to compose herself. She could easily manage the car, she told herself calmly. She was a good driver. As for Ryan . . .? She didn't dare think about that. She would face his wrath when she returned the car. The most important thing now was getting home to her child.

She reversed the car out of the garage with relative ease and was feeling quite pleased with herself as she stopped and changed gear into first.

'Heather, for God's sake get out of that car!' Ryan's voice boomed across the courtyard making her jump. Her eyes flicked upwards to the driving mirror just in time to see him dismounting his horse behind her and striding towards the car with long, angry strides.

She swallowed nervously. Ryan didn't look as if he was in any mood to argue with—in fact, he looked as if he was going to lift her bodily from the car. Without stopping to think, she put her foot down on the accelerator and the car shot forward, purring down the long drive at an effortless speed.

Heather shivered, feeling ice-cold with nerves and fear. Her hands were gripping the steering-wheel with such fierce tension that the knuckles gleamed white. She shouldn't be doing this, an inner voice warned her. Ryan was not a man to tolerate anyone going against his direct orders. But she kept on going, keeping Sarah's face firmly to the forefront of her mind. She was only a baby and Heather knew that she would be fretting for her now. She wouldn't be able to understand why her mother wasn't there when she was feeling so ill. What if she was seriously ill? The doctor might be admitting her into a hospital at this very minute.

The blaring of a car horn intruded sharply into her thoughts and she glanced in the mirror to see Ryan's Lamborghini was directly behind her. 'Damn!' She bit anxiously on her lower lip, wondering what she should do now. There was no chance that she would be able to speed away from such a powerful car. Glancing ahead, she could see the entrance gates looming and, as the housekeeper had told her, they were firmly closed. By the time she had stopped and pressed the remote control that opened them Ryan would have dragged her forcibly from the driving seat.

He was flashing his headlights at her now, and suddenly he was accelerating to come adjacent to her, the window on his passenger side gliding smoothly down as he shouted something across to her. She couldn't hear what he was saying and with a sigh she started to put her foot on the brake. It was no good, she was going to have to stop the car.

Only the car wouldn't stop! Terrified, Heather pumped madly on the brake pedal. It slowed the car a little bit, but not nearly enough, and the gates were approaching with frightening rapidity. Her brain seemed to freeze with panic and she glanced helplessly across at Ryan. He was signalling for her to wind down her window and with shaking hands she quickly obeyed.

'Slow it down through the gears, honey.' His calm orders somehow managed to restore her brain from the petrified fear that had frozen it. Her heart thudded madly as she followed his instructions, her hand poised over the handbrake so that she could pull it on at just the right moment.

'Now swing your wheel around to the left.'

The sharp, authoritative voice was left behind as she complied. The car swing violently sideways before coming to an abrupt halt with the rear of the car smashing against a tree.

The noise shattered the quietness of the countryside with startling force, a few birds fluttered from the tree in alarm, and then there was only silence and mercifully for Heather the darkness of unconsciousness.

'Heather.' The deep, familiar voice seemed to be coming from a great distance and she struggled to open her eyes.

She was lying on the hard, cold ground, something soft under her head, and she frowned, trying to remember where she was, what she was doing here.

'Heather?' The voice spoke her name again, and there was a deep note of anxiety now in the rich timbre of its tone. This time her eyelashes flickered up and she stared at the blurred image of a man; his dark hair and tanned skin swam dizzily in front of her.

'Are you all right?' A gentle hand touched her face, before moving down to her body in a rapid exploration of her arms and legs.

With the sure touch of his hands everything came sharply back into focus and she stared at Ryan with wide dark eyes in a face that was devoid of any colour. 'Don't . . . don't touch me!' Her voice had a sharp, hysterical note to it and his mouth twisted drily, the concern leaving his blue eyes with swift ease.

'Obviously you are all right,' he muttered.

She struggled to sit up and he put a strong arm around her for support. 'Stop it.' She pushed him away harshly and got unsteadily up on to her feet.

The whole world tilted and then seemed to somersault in a weird mixture of colours, as if she were looking through a kaleidoscope. She swayed and would have fallen except for Ryan catching her and holding her close.

She clung to him, burying her head against his chest, squeezing her eyes tightly closed until the dizziness seemed to pass. Then she twisted her head sideways and opened her eyes, still leaning weakly against him.

The first thing she saw was Ryan's car. The once beautiful gleaming red Alfa had its complete back wing crunched up against a tree. She groaned. 'Oh, God, Ryan, I'm . . . I'm sorry.' She turned her head in again, feeling the reassuring warmth of his body radiating out towards her. 'Your lovely car!' She swallowed and clung tightly. 'I didn't mean to do it, the brakes wouldn't work. I'll . . .' she was rambling almost incoherently '. . . I'll pay for the damage,' she finished lamely.

He held her a little way away from him and stared down at her with deep, unfathomable eyes. She was crying, she realised suddenly! Tears were streaming down her face and clinging to her long dark eyelashes. He reached out a hand and touched her forehead, making her wince sharply away.

'You've cut your head,' he muttered. 'You're damn lucky you didn't kill yourself.'

'I'm sorry.' Heather wiped her tears away with the back of her hand. 'Honestly I am.' She looked up at him with dark, pleading eyes.

'I know,' was all he said, and there was no hint of anger in his calm voice.

Heather stared at him, perplexed. She had just smashed an expensive car and she had taken it without his permission. She expected some harsh words, but none came.

'Come on, we had better get you back to the house and ring a doctor.' Ryan picked up his jacket from the ground, one hand still holding her arm.

His mention of the doctor brought all Heather's anxieties rushing back. She had to get home to her daughter; she had no time to waste getting a doctor for herself. 'Ryan, I've got to go home,' she sobbed. 'Please, please, take me home.'

For a moment he held her close against his hard body, his hand soothing against the silk of her hair. Then abruptly he was swinging her up off her feet and carrying her towards his Lamborghini. She curled her hands up around his neck, closing her eyes as she breathed in the tangy fresh scent of his cologne. It was a delicious, elusive scent that was warm and familiar from the past; it helped her to relax. Ryan would take her home, he would take care of everything in that calm, capable way of his.

She felt cold when he placed her gently down into the comfortable seat of his car, and strangely bereft. She wanted the reassuring warmth of Ryan's body.

When he got in behind the steering-wheel she leaned her head sideways against his shoulder. Her eyes felt strangely heavy as she watched him start the car with sure, swift movements.

'Everything will be all right now.' Was that small, trembling voice hers? Her eyes started to flicker closed. She felt so tired, she didn't know what was wrong with her, but she didn't seem able to keep her eyes open.

'Don't fall asleep on me, Heather.' Ryan's voice held

a sharp note that made her eyes fly open. 'I think you might have a slight concussion.'

'No, there's nothing wrong with me.' She frowned at the sluggish note to her voice. 'I've got to go home.'

'Yes, I know, but first it's back to my home so I can get you checked over by my doctor.'

'No!' Heather sat up swiftly and then wished that she hadn't as pain shot through her head. She grimaced and slowly rested back down against him.

'I will take you home just as soon as my mind is put at rest that you're OK.' He lifted one hand from the steering-wheel to stroke her head gently. She had lost the grip that had secured her hair, and it was loose and wildly disordered around her small face. The touch of his hand running so gently through it was wonderful, and she cuddled closer, absorbing the pleasure of being close to him.

'I was going to take you earlier. I'd changed my mind and returned to the house when I saw you in that car.' He took a deep breath and she realised that even though he seemed so calm the incident had shocked him. 'I tried to tell you to get out of it. I knew the braking system was faulty—that was why I took the keys away so no one could use it till it was fixed. I think my whole life flashed before my eyes when you just took off in it like that.'

She squeezed her eyes tightly closed. 'I am sorry, Ryan. I don't think I was thinking straight, I was just so desperate to leave.'

'Obviously.' He pulled the car to a halt by the side door of the house, before turning in his seat to put his other arm around her shoulder. 'Was that because of last night? If so I——'

'No, nothing to do with that,' she cut across him

quickly. She didn't even want to think about that incident, not now when he was holding her so tenderly, making her feel safe and protected. Somehow her guard was slipping—nothing seemed important except her daughter and the strong arms that held her. 'I wanted to go home because of Sarah.'

'And who is Sarah?' he asked in a quiet, perplexed voice.

'She . . . she's my daughter.' Heather stammered a little over the words and she couldn't lift her head to look at him.

For a moment there was a startled silence. 'I see,' Ryan said at last. 'You seem to have been holding out on me, haven't you, Heather?' He released his hold on her abruptly and she was forced to sit up and look at him.

'No!' Her voice was horrified now as the reality of what she had just said struck her forcefully. What on earth had possessed her to say that? If he guessed the truth now . . .? Her body froze with terror at the mere thought.

'Why didn't you tell me you had a child?' he asked at last, a deep frown furrowing his brow as he stared into her dark eyes.

'Because . . . because . . .' She was stumbling, her thoughts confused, unsure. 'Because I didn't think the fact would interest you.' She turned away from those bright, watchful eyes. 'Because my personal life doesn't really concern you,' she added dully.

'No, I suppose not,' he muttered. 'But I find it strange that you seem to have kept it such a closely guarded secret.'

'Not really. The people at work know all about Sarah,' she assured him quickly, trying to get rid of the suspicious light in those eyes. He was making her feel very nervous.

'So it's only a secret from me?' Before she could make any reply to that he had turned swiftly to climb out of the car.

Heather's heart thudded wildly as she watched him walk around towards her door. He looked as if he was deep in thought and her hands curled into tight fists at her side as she wondered frantically what was running through his mind.

Ryan had to help her into the house. Her whole body felt stiff and very sore—probably a reaction from shock, she realised.

Mrs Marton met them in the hall, her face lined with worry as she caught sight of Heather.

'It's all right, Mrs Marton,' Ryan reassured her quickly. 'She has just grazed her head slightly, but ring for a doctor so we can be on the safe side.'

The housekeeper nodded and hurried away to do as he had asked.

'I would rather you didn't do this,' Heather protested weakly as he brought her into the lounge and helped her down on to the settee. 'Can't I just go home now?'

'All in good time,' came the infuriating answer.

'But I don't want to waste time waiting for a doctor,' Heather wailed at him. 'I'll be much better when I get back to my own apartment.'

'Why this terrible rush?' Ryan enquired lazily. 'Suppose you tell me what the problem is with your daughter?'

Was it her imagination, Heather wondered anxiously, or had he given a peculiar emphasis to the word 'your'?

'She's ill and she needs me.' She desperately tried to keep the panic out of her voice.

'What's the matter with her?'

Heather shrugged. 'Susan, that is, the child-minder I employ, she rang this morning to say that her temperature was way up and she was looking feverish.'

'Well, I'm sure Susan is capable of dealing with the situation and calling for a doctor,' Ryan told her reassuringly. 'I take it she is a qualified child-minder?'

'Yes,' Heather agreed dully, and then buried her head in her hands. 'But you don't understand. I should be there—Sarah is only a baby, she needs me.' She could feel the tears prickling the back of her eyelids. 'I should never have left her; it's all my fault. I knew she wasn't well before I came away.' Her voice was thick with distress and recrimination. 'Oh, God, Ryan, I don't know what I'll do if something happens to her.'

'Nothing is going to happen to her.' Ryan sat down next to her and put a soothing arm around her. 'Come on, Heather, this isn't like you. Pull yourself together.'

How did he know what was like her? She sniffed loudly. He wouldn't understand a mother's fierce love for her child. He wouldn't understand her need to be with her daughter, to protect her and cherish her, keeping all harm at bay. Ryan would never understand a love like that. She sniffed again and Ryan took a handkerchief from his pocket and handed it to her. She took it gratefully, dabbing at the tears that shimmered in her eyes.

'How old is Sarah?' The question was asked casually, but Heather felt her whole body stiffen.

'Only three,' she mumbled into the linen handkerchief, deliberately not referring to the fact that Sarah was four next week. God, how on earth had she got herself into this situation? She should never have come here; she should have stuck firmly to her resolve and refused to come. She rubbed her eyes furiously hard.

'Don't do that.' Ryan pulled the handkerchief firmly away and stared at her. She felt almost naked under that intense gaze. I'm sure he knows, she thought wildly. I'm sure he's guessed.

'I'll bring the phone over and you can ring and check up that everything is all right,' he said softly, getting up.

She nodded, relief in her dark eyes. No, he didn't know—how could he? It was just her guilty conscience that made her feel like this. She frowned at that thought. Why should she feel guilty? Ryan had never been in love with her; he wouldn't have wanted to be stuck with her and a baby. It didn't make sense for her to feel guilty.

'The thing that puzzles me, Heather, is why didn't you tell me about Sarah this morning at the stables? You know if you'd told me the truth I would have taken you home directly.' Ryan's soft voice made her head jerk back and for a moment they just stared silently at each other, Heather's heart pounding wildly in the tense silence.

To Heather's intense relief Mrs Marton came back at that moment with a tray of tea. 'The doctor is on his way,' she informed them, seemingly unaware of the atmosphere in the room.

'Thank you, and I'm sorry I've caused all this trouble.' Heather took the delicate china cup gratefully and sipped at the hot contents. It was very sweet and she grimaced.

'You need hot sweet tea,' Mrs Marton told her in a no-nonsense voice. 'You've had a shock.'

You can say that again, Heather thought wryly. He knows, I'm sure he knows.

'Better do as you are told.' Ryan grinned, making her

reverse her opinions all over again. He passed the phone over towards her. 'Here, phone home. I guarantee that it will make you feel better.'

They left her alone to make her call, a fact for which Heather was very thankful. Her hand trembled a little as she dialled her number. Please let Sarah be all right, she prayed silently as the phone started to ring.

Susan wasn't long in answering it. 'The doctor is here now, Ms Edwards. He says there's nothing to worry about,' she told her quickly. 'Would you like to speak to him?'

Heather closed her eyes in grateful relief. 'Yes, please.'

'Nothing worse than a dose of flu, Mrs Edwards,' the doctor told her briskly. 'Probably made worse by nerves and the excitement of your being away. I've written a prescription for her.'

Heather stared at the phone absently after she put it down. The doctor had said Sarah's condition had been made worse by the fact that she was not there. She bit her lip, guilt flooding through her. She should never have left her, never. What sort of a mother was she, to have gone away when her child was ill? What sort of mother was she at all? She was hardly ever at home; she was always leaving her child with some stranger. Not that Susan wasn't a lovely girl, and she did a good job. But was that really any consolation when she was missing out on her daughter's growing up, and her daughter was missing both a mother and a father?

Heather was very quiet as Ryan drove her back to Manchester an hour later. She was still consumed with guilt over Sarah, and now, to add to that, she was worried about Ryan taking her home.

He would probably come inside with her when they

arrived because her body was stiff and still painful, and she found it difficult to walk. The doctor had said it was just the aftermath of shock and told her to rest. Ryan was certainly going to insist on helping her inside. What if he should see Sarah? He would know when he looked at his daughter that she was his. There was no mistaking those blue eyes, that gleam of copper in her dark hair—even some of her facial expressions were so like her father's.

Ryan pulled the car up outside her apartment and she turned dark-shadowed eyes on him. 'Thank you, Ryan.' Her voice was hoarse with fear. 'And I'm sorry about this morning and your car. I'll pay for the damage.'

He was watching her closely. 'Let's get you inside, shall we?' was his only reply, and Heather's heart started to thump wildly.

'I'm . . . I'm sure I can manage from here,' she told him hastily. She opened the door and slid sideways, struggling to get out.

Ryan came around with an unhurried, casual ease and helped her out. 'I don't think you can,' he told her drily. He put an arm around her waist and she had no choice but to lean on him. He was right, she couldn't manage all the steps up to her apartment on her own.

Her hands trembled as she took out her front door key when they finally reached their destination; she shook so much that it dropped on to the floor and Ryan bent to pick it up. With a wry glance at her, he opened the door himself.

The apartment was warm and welcoming, and Heather gave a sigh of relief as she stepped inside. Maybe Ryan would go now.

Susan came out into the hall, her glance going first to the darkly handsome man who had his arm around her employer's waist. Then her eyes moved to Heather, noting with shock the bandage which the doctor had put on her forehead. 'What on earth has happened? Are you all right, Ms Edwards?'

'It's a long story, Susan.' Heather tried to disentangle herself from Ryan. 'But I'm fine now.'

'Let's just say she was a little too anxious to get home,' Ryan put in with a grin.

Susan grimaced in concern and then her eyes rested again on Ryan's broad-shouldered frame with considerable interest.

'Well, I think you can go now, Ryan, and thank you once again,' Heather cut in impatiently.

Ryan's eyebrows rose slightly. 'I thought you might at least offer me a cup of tea.' He smiled his most charming smile at the girl in front of him, and Heather noticed how she blushed and looked totally bemused.

'Of course I will go and make you one.' Susan almost fell over herself in her eagerness to please. 'Would you like one, Ms Edwards?'

Heather hesitated. She didn't know what to say—all she knew was that she didn't want Ryan here. It was far too dangerous. But she could hardly refuse him a cup of tea; it would look decidedly odd. She nodded resignedly and then waved Ryan in towards the lounge. She waited for him to move towards the other room before turning towards Sarah's door. This was a nightmare.

'Mumma!' Sarah squealed in excitement and held up her arms. Her little face was pale, making her eyes look like huge saucers in her face, and her dark hair was loose around the fluffy rabbit pyjamas.

Heather had to swallow on a lump in her throat as she held her daughter tightly against her, cuddling the warm little body and kissing the upturned face.

'Are you all right, honey?' she asked anxiously as she pulled away to examine the little girl more closely.

'Yes, I had to have the doctor and——Oh!' Sarah stopped suddenly as she noticed the bandage on Heather's forehead. 'What's happened to your head?'

'It's nothing, darling, just a little bump.' Heather dismissed it quickly. 'Now what did the doctor say to you?'

'He said I was too old to cry,' Sarah answered solemnly.

'Were you crying?' Heather stroked the dark hair gently back from the small face.

'Only a little,' Sarah admitted in a brave tone. 'The doctor said when you get to four years of age you're too old to cry.'

'Did he?' Heather's voice was soft. 'Well, you're not quite four yet, so that's all right.'

There was a tap on the door behind them and Heather turned, thinking it would be Susan with some tea. The door was pushed open and someone came in carrying a tray—only it wasn't Susan, it was Ryan.

'Well, now, are mother and daughter doing all right?' he asked with a wry twist of his lips.

Heather could hardly find her voice to answer him. She was horrified and completely paralysed with fear.

Ryan didn't seem to notice her white face, the dark stricken eyes, as he came further into the room. He put the tray down on the bedside table before looking at Sarah. 'How's the invalid?' he asked her. His voice was light and there was a teasing grin on his lips, but his eyes were piercing in their intent as they moved over the little girl's face.

Sarah was taken aback for a moment and she

frowned. She wasn't used to men, and she wasn't sure about this stranger who had suddenly walked into her bedroom. So she didn't answer him.

'Dear me!' Ryan drawled with a charming ease. 'This is a terrible thing—someone has stolen Sarah's voice. Who could have done such a wicked thing?' His eyes moved to Heather and there was a cold glint in their blue depths as they raked over her ashen face.

Sarah giggled. 'Nobody, I had it all the time.'

'You did?' Ryan's attention was quickly back on the little girl. 'Well, you really had me fooled.'

'How did you know my name?' the little girl enquired, her eyes wide and alert.

'Oh, I know everything,' Ryan said in a deep voice, making Sarah laugh again.

'You must be magic, like the people in my story-books.'

'I think, sweetheart, that you should get some rest now,' Heather managed to insert. Her mouth was dry and her heart was pumping madly.

'Oh, do I have to?' Sarah wrinkled her nose.

'Afraid so.' Heather moved to tuck her in, anxious to get Ryan out of the room as soon as possible.

'Aren't you going to read me a story?' The little girl's lips quivered slightly.

'A little later, when Mr Jameson has gone home.' Heather deliberately used Ryan's surname in a bid to keep everything on an impersonal note.

'Goodnight, Sarah,' Ryan murmured from beside her.

The child turned to stare up at him. 'It's not night-time,' she told him with a grin. 'So you see, you don't know everything.'

'Bet I do.' Ryan smiled. 'Bet I know how old you are.'

Heather's eyes flew to his dark, impassive face, her

heart thundering madly. 'Now come on, you two!' she said with a tremble in her voice. 'We have no time for this nonsense.'

Ryan flashed her a disdainful glance which silenced her abruptly. 'I bet you are four years of age,' he said quietly, his eyes never leaving Heather's face. He watched drily as her complexion flared up to a brilliant red and then back to pure snow-white.

'No!' Sarah shouted with glee. 'See, you don't know everything.'

Ryan frowned for a moment, the gleam leaving his eyes to stare down at the child.

Heather started to breathe again and made to turn for the door. 'Coming, Ryan?' she asked quietly.

He moved to follow her and then glanced back at Sarah. She grinned at him impishly. 'I'm not four until Friday.' She chuckled gleefully.

Heather could feel the blood draining away from her body; the panic she felt was almost terror. Ryan moved past her and the look he bestowed on her chilled her to the very core.

'Mumma, you haven't kissed me like you usually do,' Sarah complained from her bed.

For once Heather didn't answer her daughter. She couldn't move; she couldn't speak.

'Don't be long, Heather,' Ryan grated harshly from the doorway. 'I'll be waiting for you in the lounge.'

She sank down on to the bed as the door closed. He knew . . . Ryan knew the truth. Her body trembled wretchedly. She felt sick inside and hugged her arms around her middle. The one thing in the world that she had most feared had happened . What would Ryan say? What would he do?

'Are you all right, Mumma?' Sarah asked anxiously.

'Yes, of course.' She kissed the child's warm little

cheek and then got numbly to her feet. She had to go in and see him; she had to get this over with.

She closed Sarah's bedroom door quietly and moved slowly towards the lounge. Her head was throbbing madly, yet it was nothing compared with the pain that was splintering inside her as she went into that room to face him.

CHAPTER SEVEN

RYAN was standing with his back towards Heather, staring at the gold-framed photographs of Sarah that were hanging above the long antique bureau. Heather bit her lip; had he seen those photographs when he came in here to wait for her? Had that been what had prompted him to go into Sarah's bedroom?

He turned suddenly to look across the room at her. His tall, powerful body was a silhouette against the window behind him and it was difficult to see the expression on his face. Yet an aura of intimidating menace seemed to radiate from him. It was there in the hard lines of his body, the aggressive thrust of his chin. Heather felt sick with fear.

'You have a very lovely daughter.' The calm steadiness of his voice bewildered her and she just continued to stare at him. The full light from the window was flooding over her; she knew he would be able to note the merest flicker of her eyelash. 'She looks a little like you, but I guess there is a lot of her father in her.'

Heather leaned weakly against the soft chintz upholstery of the armchair beside her. How should she play this? she wondered desperately. His tone and his turn of phrase sounded innocuous enough, yet she knew he was toying with her, just waiting to move in for the kill.

'What do you think, Heather—is she anything like her father?' he prompted in a silky tone she didn't much care for.

114

'A little.' Her voice sounded husky and she swallowed convulsively.

'Only a little?' There was a curling edge to his voice now. 'I notice you're not displaying any photographs of father and daughter together.' He jerked his head disdainfully back towards the pictures.

'Well, I . . .' She licked her lips nervously and started again. 'Now that Jonathan is dead I find them painful to——'

'Cut the hypocrisy, Heather,' he intervened in a harsh tone. 'I can't bear to listen to it. That grieving widow act of yours turns my stomach.'

Heather's heart thundered wildly, how much had he guessed?

'The only thing that would pain you is the fact that Edwards obviously hasn't left you in the style to which you would like to become accustomed.' He flung a scathing look around the comfortable room which was furnished tastefully, but without any wild extravagance. 'How could you do it, Heather?' he asked at last, his voice a low growl in the deep silence.

Heather shook her head helplessly. Sometimes in her wildest nightmares she had thought about this very scene, but she had always calmed herself with the thought that she would just tell him in a dispassionate, self-possessed way that Sarah was her late husband's child. Faced with the reality, those two emotions were nowhere in sight and she knew she would never be able to tell him such a cold-blooded, blatant lie.

'Damn it, answer me!' Ryan barked suddenly. 'Don't you think I had the right to know my own daughter?'

There it was, the question she had always dreaded. Surprisingly it didn't make her fall to pieces. The tone of his voice, the arrogant assumption of his rights made her head snap upwards angrily. 'You don't have any rights, Ryan,' she told him in a voice that shook with emotion.

'Like hell I don't!' He moved swiftly across the room, catching her by the forearms in a vice-like grip. 'Sarah is my flesh and blood. She is mine and that gives me every right in the world.' He shook her and Heather winced with pain at the pressure of his strong arms.

'You're hurting me, Ryan!' she cried softly. She was frightened as she looked up at those harsh, dark features. She had never seen Ryan so angry, so out of control.

'Why didn't you tell me you were pregnant?' he demanded fiercely.

She was helpless in the wake of his anger. 'Because you were leaving to go to the States, because our relationship, or "our affair" as you like to call it, was over.' There was a catch in her choked voice, tears so close to escaping. 'I didn't think there was any point in telling you; I didn't think you would be interested.'

For a moment he looked at her as if he would like to physically strike her. Then he moved back, his hands clenched into tight fists at his sides, an expression of iron calm crossing his face. 'That is the most contemptuous assumption it has ever been your misfortune to make,' he told her coldly. For a moment he watched her, his eyes glittering with livid blue light, and she could almost see his mind working, see him thinking everything through in that clear, decisive way of his.

'That day when you came to the airport to see me off, I knew there was something. I thought . . .' His voice trailed off suddenly. 'Well, it doesn't matter what I thought.' He glared at her.

She couldn't bear the icy condemnation in those eyes

and she buried her face in her hands for a moment before raking them through the long silken strands of her hair in a gesture that was almost one of despair.

'No wonder you look guilty,' Ryan continued in a harsh, brittle tone. 'I don't know how you can look me in the face,' he jeered.

'I have nothing to feel guilty about,' Heather retorted, her voice rising fiercely. 'We didn't love each other. You made it clear that you weren't interested when you left for the States. I love Sarah and I have brought her up the best way I could, which hasn't been easy, let me tell you,' she finished in a trembling voice. Her eyes darkened with the shadows of remembrance. All those long, lonely nights when she had sat nursing Sarah through all her childish ailments, then racing to work the next morning exhausted and overwrought with anxiety. The responsibility of it all had weighed heavily on her. She had worried that she couldn't give Sarah any more of her time, fretted that she might not be able to afford to buy her everything she needed if the bills were too high the next month. Being a single parent had been damned hard and she was not going to start apologising for it.

'Oh, I'm sure it hasn't been easy,' Ryan sneered. 'You know, I often wondered why you rushed so quickly into marriage after I left; now I know the truth.' His eyes were hard, his mouth twisted in a cruel line. 'The pieces of the jigsaw are falling into place, and it's not a pretty picture.'

'I don't know what you are talking about.' Heather shook her head in bewilderment.

'Oh, don't start giving me those "innocent little girl" looks—we both know what a sham they are,' Ryan grated. 'As soon as you heard I was selling up my companies you thought I was in financial difficulties. That was why you could hardly wait for me to leave before rushing into Edwards' arms. You made the mistake of thinking him a much better catch, didn't you, Heather? You set your sights on Edwards and you had to move fast because of the baby. You made a bad mistake, you grossly miscalculated.'

Heather stared at him, utterly horrified. 'You really think I would stoop so low as to pass my child off as another man's just to trap him?' She sank down in the chair beside her, limbs too weak to support her, all colour draining from her face.

'Cut the acting, Heather, it doesn't work with me. You waltzed off with Edwards the first night I was away in the States. You allowed him to give my child his name and, by God, that isn't something I am going to tolerate or forgive.'

She flinched as he reached out a hand to capture her chin, but his touch was menacingly gentle as he tipped her pale, oval face upwards. 'You thought you were being very clever, didn't you?' he murmured, and his thumb moved upwards in a silk-like caress over the fullness of her lips, making her shiver. 'But nobody plays me for a fool and gets away with it.'

Heather tried to shake his hand away, her eyes as dark as velvet night as she stared up at him. 'What do you intend to do?' she whispered, tension etching itself visibly over her young face.

He smiled; it was a cruel smile, one that was confident and certain of its domination. 'I'm going to take what's mine, of course,' he told her lightly. Then he released her abruptly and swung out of the room and out of the apartment, closing the door with a quietness that was terrifying.

Heather didn't know how long she sat there staring into space, her mind racing in circles, her body shivering. What had he meant by that last statement? Did he intend to try and take Sarah from her? Was that it? He could never do that, she thought with wild panic. Never!

She groaned and buried her head in her hands. Deep in her heart she had always known that Ryan would want his child. She had never been able to admit the truth as openly as this to herself before, but she had always been aware of it. He hadn't wanted her, but his child, his flesh and blood—that was different. Sarah belonged to him, it was a question of pride that she should bear his name, be under his control. There was no sentiment or love attached to his reasoning; the point at issue was Ryan's self-esteem.

She had thought that changing her name, assuming the identity of a widow, would give her a safety barrier to hide behind should she ever be faced with this situation. Inadvertently she had just made matters much worse. Now Ryan believed that she had cheated him out of his child, allowed another man to give Sarah his name.

She shuddered as she thought of the look of raw rage on his face. She had insulted his male sense of honour and she knew he would stop at nothing until he felt it was restored. If that meant taking Sarah away from her, then he would find a way to do it. He was rich enough and powerful enough for anything.

For a moment her tortured mind conjured up images of Ryan and Annabel bringing up her daughter. Annabel had told her that she was going to marry him. She felt a stab of almost uncontrollable jealousy and fear when she thought of that woman taking her child. 'Stop it,

Heather,' she told herself harshly. 'You are being ridiculous, that could never happen.' But could it? a little voice asked inside. Even if Ryan couldn't get Sarah on a permanent basis he could get access and visitation rights. That could mean Sarah spending weekends with him and Annabel. Heather bit so sharply on her lip that she could taste blood.

'Are you all right, Ms Edwards?' Susan's voice jerked her away from her appaling conjecture and she glanced up; she had forgotten all about Susan's being in the apartment! Had she heard anything of that dreadful argument? she wondered.

'Yes, I'm fine. My head is hurting a little,' she managed to say, hoping that would explain to the girl why she was sitting with her head in her hands.

'I'm just going to get Sarah's prescription from the chemist; is there anyting you want while I'm there?'

Heather shook her head. 'No, all I need is rest, thanks, Susan.' If only that were all she needed, she thought wryly. If only she could go to sleep and wake up with everything back to normal.

'The man that brought you home is very handsome, isn't he?' Susan chatted happily as she buttoned up her coat.

'Yes, very,' Heather agreed without much enthusiasm.'He usually makes an impression on women.'

'Young and old alike.' Susan smiled. 'I just popped my head around Sarah's door and she was singing his praises. She calls him "Mr Magic".'

'Does she?' Heather's voice rose drily, but Susan didn't seem to notice anything amiss.

'I won't be long,' she said, hurrying towards the door.

'Mr Magic,' Heather repeated into the silence of the

room. 'The man who is capable of anything.'

Heather phoned into work sick on Monday morning. She couldn't face going into the office; not only was her head hurting, but she felt too tense and miserable to be able to face anyone or concentrate on work.

'I had a slight accident and I'm still feeling a bit shaky,' she told Robert Craven, and he made the necessary sounds of sympathy before getting to the real point of interest.

'How did the weekend go? Do you think we have definitely got the contract?'

'Hard to say,' Heather murmured non-committally. 'There wasn't much time to discuss anything.'

'Well, didn't he give you any indication?' Robert grated impatiently. 'Surely you could have got something out of him?'

Nothing that you would be pleased to hear about, Heather thought drily. 'I'm sure he will be in contact some time today,' she told him soothingly.

'Mmm, and meanwhile you are off work,' Robert muttered in a tone that suggested that she might be malingering, which was unfair considering she rarely had a day off sick. 'How long do you think you'll be off?'

'I don't know—a couple of days maybe,' she answered vaguely. 'I cut my head and I'm suffering from a slight migraine.'

'How the hell did you manage to do that anyway?' he asked suddenly.

'I bashed it against the side of a car . . . Look, Robert, I have to go now,' Heather said hastily. 'I'll ring you tomorrow and keep you informed.' She replaced the receiver quickly and let out a sigh. She couldn't have told her boss that she had hurt her head when she crashed a prospective client's car; he would probably have had a coronary right there and then.

She leaned wearily back against the pillows of her bed. Nothing was going right for her. She hadn't been able to sleep for the last couple of nights, she was so worried. It wouldn't surprise her now if Ryan decided against giving the contract to Craven's. He was out to hurt her and he would do that any way he could.

'Mumma.' Sarah came running into the bedroom. She looked a lot better this morning; her temperature was down and her skin was back to its normal creamy colour. 'I think my dolly is sick,' she said in a grave voice, holding out a battered-looking doll that was an old favourite. 'Do you think we should call the doctor?'

Heather took the doll and pretended to examine it. 'No, I think she will be all right.' She smiled. 'But I think we should put some clothes on the poor thing; she looks a bit cold.'

Sarah nodded her head, her eyes bright and alert.

'But first, young lady,' Heather swung the child up beside her and cuddled her close, 'let's get you out of those pyjamas and dressed.'

Once Heather had got Sarah washed and dressed in a pink dungaree suit with her hair neatly braided, she showered and put on a pair of faded denims and a midnight-blue cashmere jumper.

It was lovely being able to take her time over breakfast with Sarah. Usually Monday mornings were such a rush, with only time to snatch a coffee and give Sarah a quick kiss on the way out. If only she didn't have all these distressing thoughts pressing down on her she would have enjoyed this day.

She watched Sarah closely as they sat in the lounge

later doing a small jigsaw. She was really growing up and she looked so like her father. Those beautiful china-blue eyes fringed by the long sweep of dark lashes—she even had the same small cleft in her chin that dimpled so delightfully when she smiled. Heather felt a painful tug at her heart. If only things had been different, if only Ryan had loved her. Things would have been so wonderful. They would be together, Sarah would have a father, Heather would have the one man who had made her feel alive. For a moment she remembered the touch of his hand against her skin, the warmth of his breath against the vulnerable curve of her neck, the heady scent of his male cologne. Such little things, yet just thinking about them made her ache inside.

There was a sudden ring at the doorbell and Heather jumped nervously. Would that be Ryan? She felt sure that she would hear from him some time today.

'Shall I go?' Susan called from the kitchen where she was making them some lunch.

'Please.' Unconsciously Heather held her breath as she watched the lounge door. Part of her wanted it to be him, yet another side of her was terrified of seeing him.

When the door opened, however, it was Richard who came in, not Ryan. His arms were filled with a huge bouquet of flowers.

'Richard, how nice!' Heather's voice gushed with mingled relief and disappointment.

'Thought I'd pop over in my lunch-hour and see how the invalid is progressing.' He smiled, his grey eyes crinkling at the corners as he noticed Sarah sitting beside her. 'Hi, there,' he said pleasantly to her.

'Hi,' Sarah murmured. She knew Richard Craven—he had been to the apartment once or twice when he had accompanied Heather on business dinners. He wasn't exactly a stranger to her, yet her manner was quiet and wary.

'I brought you a few flowers.' Richard put the bouquet down on the coffee-table as if he were embarrassed by them.

'They're lovely, thank you.' Heather inclined her head to the settee behind him. 'Why don't you sit down? I'll ask Susan to make you some tea.'

'Thanks.' Richard grinned and sat down, raking a nervous hand through thick blond hair. 'How are you feeling?'

'Better,' Heather answered. 'Still a bit sore, though.'

Susan came in and Heather smiled at her. 'Would you mind making Richard some tea?'

'Of course not.' She moved to pick up the flowers. 'I'll put these in water for you,' she offered shyly, sending a quick glance at Richard before leaving the room.

Richard watched her go with a light of interest in his grey eyes. 'Pretty girl,' he murmured when the door closed.

'Yes,' Heather agreed with a grin. 'And unattached.'

Richard's colour mounted. 'Oh, I didn't mean . . .' He stumbled to a halt and Heather took pity on him and changed the subject.

'How are things at the office?'

He sighed and leaned back in his seat. 'Dad is not in a good mood. He sent these over for you, by the way.' He put a file he had been carrying down in front of her.

Heather glanced through it idly. It was some work that she had been doing on Friday but hadn't finished because of her early departure. 'Doesn't like to give me a minute, does he?' she mocked lightly.

'That's Dad,' Richard agreed. 'He's asked me to deal with the Redstar thing until you get back.'

'Oh?' Heather's eyebrows rose. 'Has Ryan been in contact, then?'

Richard shook his head. 'No, and I'm not sure how to progress with it. I rang his office this morning but his secretary said he was unavailable.'

'I see.' Heather bit her lip; that certainly didn't sound too promising.

'Do you think I should go around there and try and make an appointment?'

Heather thought about that for a moment and then shook her head. 'No, leave it today. I have a feeling I'll hear from him soon, so I'll suss out the situation.'

'Fair enough,' Richard agreed. 'But I hope it's today. Dad is getting very overwrought about the whole thing.'

Susan came back with their tea and some sandwiches and the conversation turned to more trivial things until it was time for Richard to get back to work.

'You won't mind if I don't see you out?' she murmured. 'I'm supposed to be resting.'

'Not at all.' Richard stood up. 'Get better soon, Heather, won't you? We need you back at work.'

She nodded and for a moment his glance lingered gently on her, taking in the casual attire and the flow of long dark hair. 'You're looking very beautiful, by the way.'

'Thanks,' she said lightly, then as he turned towards the door she called, 'And, Richard, put your head around the kitchen door and say goodbye to Susan.' For a moment he hesitated, then, nodding, he left the room.

Heather looked at the closed door, a thoughtful expression on her face. She had noticed how he and Susan seemed to be attracted to each other. There could be a nice romance brewing there.

She turned to find Sarah watching her, her eyes wide. 'Uncle Richard thinks you are beautiful,' she said in an awed voice.

Heather laughed; she had almost forgotten Sarah was sitting there so quietly taking everything in. 'But not as beautiful as my daughter,' she said, ruffling her dark hair.

The nights were drawing in now, Heather thought later as she switched on the overhead light in the kitchen at four o'clock. Soon it would be Christmas. She wondered what sort of holiday it would be this year.

The doorbell rang and her heart leaped anxiously. 'Stay where you are,' she told Sarah, who was colouring in a book at the table. 'I'll be back in a minute.' Slowly she untied the apron that she had been wearing while baking some scones, and with unhurried steps moved towards the hall.

She glanced at herself in the mirror before opening the door. She looked flushed from the heat of the kitchen and she wore no make-up; her hair was loose in shining waves around her shoulders. She didn't look very sophisticated or poised, not someone to compare with Annabel Rothstar. Why did she wish all of a sudden that she had dressed a little more provocatively this morning?

She opened the door cautiously and, as she had expected, Ryan stood outside. He was dressed in a dark formal business suit and white shirt and he looked devastatingly attractive.

'Can I come in?' he enquired after a moment of tense silence.

She stood back. 'I'm surprised you even bother to ask

permission. I'd have thought you would have you own key to the place by now.' She couldn't help the sarcastic words; she was nervous and unsure and it seemed her only means of defence.

Surprisingly he ignored her jibe. 'How's your head?' he asked instead, his eyes flicking over her slim body, then up towards the heavy thickness of her dark hair.

'Not too bad.' She turned to lead the way back into the kitchen. They were behaving like strangers, as if that confrontation yesterday had never taken place.

'We need to talk, Heather,' he said suddenly, catching hold of her arm.

She nodded, flicking an uncertain look up at him through long, dark lashes. At least he seemed calmer today, more rational. Maybe that threat yesterday had just been made in the heat of the moment.

She pushed the kitchen door open and Sarah swung her head around, her face lighting up with excitement when she saw Ryan. 'Hi, there,' she said happily.

'Hello.' Ryan smiled at her gently. 'How are you today?' He put a hand on her dark hair and she gazed up at him, a look almost of adoration in her eyes.

Heather's lips twisted drily. Sarah's attitude towards Ryan was amazing. She had hardly said a word to Richard when he was here this morning, yet now she was bubbling over with enthusiasm.

'What do you think of my picture?' Sarah asked him, holding up her colouring book.

Ryan leaned over and studied it intently. 'Not bad,' he said at last. 'But you need to put more colour in the clown's face.'

Sarah considered that with her head to one side, and then nodded. 'Yes, I think you are right,' she decided in a very mature voice, making Ryan grin.

Heather turned away; she could feel a lump lodging itself somewhere in her throat as she watched them together. She opened the oven door behind her and pretended to be busy checking her baking.

'Mmm, nice smell in here,' Ryan remarked easily.

She turned, her cheeks rosy from the heat of the oven, her dark eyes glistening as she looked at him and then away again.

'You look very domesticated.' He smiled. 'A totally different Heather from the sophisticated one in the Craven offices.'

Heather didn't know how to answer that. Was it some sort of compliment? Her eyes returned to his tall broad frame again, watching him warily.

'Have you brought Mumma any flowers?' Sarah asked suddenly.

Ryan frowned and glanced down at her. 'No, I haven't, Sarah,' he answered, obviously puzzled by the question.

'Uncle Richard did,' Sarah chatted on, oblivious to the sudden coolness in the man who stood beside her.

'Did he now?' Ryan drawled, his eyes piercing Heather.

'Yes, and he said that she was very beautiful.' Sarah continued to colour in the clown's face in a bright, vivid red. 'Do you think she is——?' she asked innocently.

'Sarah, do stop blabbering on!' Heather cut in crossly, her colour heightening to almost the same colour as the clown's as she noticed how Ryan's eyes were travelling up over the long length of her legs and the small span of her waist to the curves of her breast.

He grinned. 'Not bad . . . not bad at all, Sarah.'

Heather glared furiously at him, but he was quite unperturbed. He reached into the top pocket of his jacket and brought out a small red box which was beautifully wrapped. 'I've brought you a small present,' he told Sarah, putting it down beside her.

She hooted in excitement and picked it up. She was in the process of tearing the paper from it when she suddenly stopped and looked uncertainly over towards her mother.

'It's all right, Sarah,' she assured her. 'You can take presents from Ryan.'

'Oh, good.' The little girl continued to tear the wrapping away.

Heather looked at Ryan's dark face. 'I've told her she isn't to accept presents from strangers,' she explained.

For a moment there was an expression on Ryan's face that she couldn't fathom. It was almost as if she had struck him. Then he glanced away from her and down towards his child. 'Why don't you take your present into the lounge, Sarah? Then your mother and I can have a little talk.'

'OK.' The little girl slipped happily down from her chair, but first she ran to her mother to show her what she had been given.

It was a beautiful gold bracelet with her name on it. It had probably cost a fortune, Heather thought disparagingly. For a moment she thought about all those expensive gifts he had given her when they lived together. She had thought they were a token of his love, but they had merely been a symbol of his possession of her.

'It's lovely, darling; be careful with it,' she murmured absently.

'Wait until I show Susan,' Sarah said happily on her way out.

'Sarah.' Her mother's voice halted her. 'Have you

said thank you to Uncle Ryan?'

The little girl swung around and shook her head.
'Thank you very much, Uncle Ryan,' she said dutifully,
and then almost as an afterthought reached up for a kiss.

'Uncle Ryan?' Ryan drawled in a contemptuous tone
as the door closed behind Sarah.

Heather thought it best to ignore what could be a very
emotive subject. 'I don't want you to give Sarah
expensive presents,' she said instead.

'I'll do what the hell I want,' he grated suddenly, his
eyes hard and unyielding. 'I've got a lot of time to catch
up on with my daughter—time that you have cheated
me out of.'

'Oh, stop it, Ryan! Stop pretending that you give a
damn!' she exclaimed suddenly.

Ryan watched her for a moment with pitying
contempt. 'You think I don't care if my own child looks
at me as if I'm a stranger? If she calls me Uncle? You
think that doesn't hurt?'

'All that hurts is your male ego,' she assured him in
a trembling voice. 'You don't care about Sarah, not
really, Oh, you'll send her expensive presents, no doubt,
and play her like a puppet on a string. Maybe you will
send a few cheques now and again, just so you think
you've got a right to dictate her life. But those things
don't make you a caring parent. You wouldn't sit up all
night with her when she's ill or worry yourself sick
about her when you're at work and can't see her. You
want to possess and control, not love,' Heather blazed,
her dark eyes gleaming with gold angry lights. 'Just as
I was once your possession, now so is Sarah.'

For a moment there was a deathly silence in the room.
'If you think that, you're wrong, Heather,' Ryan stated
tightly. 'I don't want to just be on the sidelines of Sarah's

life. She is my daughter and, despite your opinion, I do have the capacity to feel love for her. I want her under my care and protection and my roof and I'll stop at nothing to get her.'

'No!' Heather recoiled in shock, conscious of the sickening lurch of her stomach. 'You can't be serious about this!'

'Contrary to what you think, Heather, I am always serious,' he drawled, 'and I don't want Sarah subjected to a string of Uncle Richards walking in and out of her life.'

'She is not subjected to any such thing.' Heather's voice seemed to be coming from a great distance away as her mind reeled in wild confusion. This just couldn't be happening to her! 'What makes you think that the environment you have to offer is any better? What about the women that walk in and out of your life? Annabel, for instance?'

'Annabel?' He frowned and then watched her closely. 'Do I detect a hint of jealousy, Heather?'

'Of course not!' she snapped. 'I think I've made it clear that I don't give a damn about your personal life. But I will never in a million years let you take my child anywhere near that woman.'

'I see.' Ryan was quiet for a moment as he thought about her words. 'So you don't like the idea of Sarah spending any time with Annabel and I?'

'Of course I damn well don't!' Heather exploded.

'Just as I don't like the thought of Richard's having a say in my child's life,' he answered quickly.

'Richard has nothing to do with this,' Heather retorted. 'He is a business colleague—nothing more.'

'A business colleague who brings you flowers and tells you you're beautiful,' Ryan muttered contemptuously. 'I'm not stupid, Heather.'

She stared at him, defenceless against his harsh, condemnatory attitude. 'All this is getting us nowhere,' she said at last in a low, tremulous voice. 'You will never get control of Sarah. No judge in this world would take her away from me.'

'You are probably right,' he conceded, his mouth twisting in a grim line. 'But I would most likely be granted access to Sarah; have you thought of that?'

She nodded dumbly and fear was written clearly all over her young face. She had done nothing but think about it.

He watched her silently for a moment, then he raked a hand through his dark hair in a distracted manner. 'We need to sit down and discuss this in a rational, adult manner.' He glanced down at the gold watch on his wrist. 'How about having dinner with me tonight?'

The question took her by surprise and she didn't answer him immediately. He glanced over at her and his eyes narrowed impatiently. 'Look, Heather, I think it's time now that we put our personal feelings aside and think about Sarah.'

She bit her lip. He was right—the animosity between them was making matters worse. The important thing here was their child, and for her sake they should both make an effort to sort things out. 'I can't go out,' she murmured. 'I've given Susan the afternoon off and I have no baby-sitter.' She hesitated for a moment before continuing, 'But you can stay for dinner, if you want, then afterwards when I've put Sarah to bed we can talk.' She watched him with wide, uncertain eyes and was surprised to see the harsh features relax as a charming smile curved his strong mouth.

'I'd like that, Heather, thank you.'

The gentleness of his voice had a disturbing effect on her nerves. 'We're not having anything special, I'm just making lasagne and——'

'Anything you're making is fine by me,' he cut across her flustered chatter smoothly. 'As I remember, you were always a very good cook. There was that one incident when you nearly set fire to the kitchen in the London apartment, but I think that was partly my fault.' There was a gleam of amusement in his eyes as he watched her colour flare up dramatically.

She remembered that episode very vividly. She had only been living with Ryan for about a week and she had decided to cook a romantic meal for them. She had bought a new dress, black, sheer and very seductive.

The dinner had been very nearly cooked and she had just been putting the finishing touches to the intimate table set for two when Ryan had arrived home. He had taken one look at her in that dress and the dinner had been well and truly forgotten.

'Good job I noticed the smoke coming under the kitchen door.' Ryan laughed now. 'I would have hated the fire brigade to find us in that——'

'Ryan!' she snapped quickly in mortification, before he could go any further.

'Sorry.' His lips curved in a rueful smile. 'That memory just seemed to hit me from nowhere. It's quite a delicious one, though, isn't it?'

She didn't answer him; she couldn't. The memory would have been a happy one if things had worked out differently between them, but as it was she just preferred to forget things like that. They disturbed her intensely.

'I'll go and keep Sarah amused while you get on with things,' he said into the silence. 'At least there's no chance of my distracting you today.'

'No.' Her voice was hollow as she watched him leave the room, a curious sensation in the pit of her stomach. Why was it that man could build up such conflicting emotions inside her? One moment she hated him, the next . . . She shook her head and firmly turned her thoughts towards the preparation of their meal.

Usually she ate with Sarah in the kitchen, but today she set the table in the small dining-room that led off it. She covered the table with a lace cloth and her best cutlery and her hand lingered on the silver candlesticks that sat on the sideboard before she quickly rejected the idea of using them. This wasn't a romantic little get-together. Ryan was here to discuss gaining access to Sarah. She took a deep steadying breath as she thought about the enormity of the situation. She was going to have to tread very, very carefully.

CHAPTER EIGHT

WHEN Heather went into the lounge to call them for dinner, she was surprised to see Ryan sitting on the floor with his daughter. He had taken off the dark jacket of his suit and his tie, and the top buttons of his white shirt were undone. He looked completely relaxed and at home as he helped Sarah to build something with her Lego. It was a far cry from the tough businessman image that he usually presented, and for a moment it caught her off balance and she just stood and stared.

'Dinner ready?' Ryan lifted his dark head and their eyes met. She nodded and swallowed hard, wondering what on earth was wrong with her.

'Come on, Sarah, time we tidied all this away,' he said briskly, starting to pick up pieces that were scattered on the floor around them.

'Ah, just a few minutes more,' Sarah complained to her mother. 'Uncle Ryan is building me an aeroplane.'

'Well, he can finish it for you another time, darling,' Heather soothed as she walked across towards them and bent to help Ryan return everything into its box.

She stumbled a little as she straightened up, and Ryan's hand went firmly around her waist to steady her. For some crazy reason she blushed at the sudden contact with him.

'Thank you.' She pulled away from him quickly and bent to pick up Sarah in order to cover her confusion. God, she was going to have to pull herself together. She was acting like an adolescent who had a crush on him—utterly ridiculous when she didn't care for the man at all.

She could feel his eyes on her, watching her every movement as they went through into the dining-room, and she had to fight to maintain a cool, composed air. The apartment suddenly seemed too small, too intimate. Her whole body seemed to have become fiercely aware of Ryan's every move, every glance.

'Why are we eating in here, Mumma?' Sarah asked as Heather settled her into her chair.

Heather had to smile at the child's artless remark. Good job I'm not trying to impress Ryan, she thought wryly. 'Because I didn't think Uncle Ryan would want to eat in the kitchen,' she answered.

'And because it is a special occasion,' Ryan added, taking the seat opposite Heather.

'It is?' Sarah asked with wide eyes.

'Of course. It's not every day I get to have dinner with two beautiful girls,' he assured her with a grin.

Sarah giggled at that, and Heather grimaced as she went into the kitchen to get the meal. She hated him to make patronising, stupid remarks like that. He could have his pick of a hundred beautiful women to dine with, or do anything else with for that matter.

She stood in the kitchen for a moment and tried to gather herself together. What on earth was wrong with her? He had simply made a light, joking remark and she was flaring up out of all proportion.

When she returned to the dining-room, Ryan had placed the silver candlesticks in the centre of the table and had lit them. It gave the room an intimate glow that at once put Heather's nerves on edge.

'You don't mind, do you, Heather, but Sarah wanted the candles?' He gave the child a conspiratorial wink and she nodded her head quickly in agreement.

'No, why should I mind?' Heather tried to keep her voice light as she served the meal and sat down opposite him.

'I'm going to have four candles on my birthday cake,' Sarah told him suddenly, in a very serious tone. 'When is your birthday, Uncle Ryan?'

'August, I've already had it,' he told her with a smile.

'How many candles did you have on your cake?' the child asked with innocent curiosity.

That made Ryan really laugh. It was a lovely deep, velvety sound that was quite infectious. 'More than I care to remember,' he told her with a shake of his head.

Heather smiled across at him, her eyes moving over the rugged handsome features, and her heart started to beat in a wild and irregular way. Quite suddenly she knew what was bothering her. It was this relaxed, casual air Ryan had about him. That lazy attractiveness that was so at variance with the tough man he really was. Dressed like that, the white shirt unbuttoned slightly giving a glimpse of dark hair on the broad chest, his tie discarded and his face softened by laughter, he reminded her very forcibly of the man she had fallen in love with.

He met her eyes across the table. Deep and unwavering, his seemed to see right into her very soul, and she looked hurriedly away and down towards the table.

'Is your meal all right?' she asked him, more for something to say to cover her confusion than anything else.

'Perfect.' He reached across and picked up the bottle of wine to refill her glass and she frowned. She didn't remember anything about drinking that first glass. She was going to have to be careful—she needed to keep all her wits about her if she was to deal with the conversation they were to have later.

Sarah didn't want to go to bed after the meal; she was having too good a time.

'Sorry, sweetheart, but it's your bedtime and you've got to go,' Heather told her firmly. 'But if you're a good girl and come now I'll read you a short story.'

'All right, then.' The child slipped down from her chair and then ran around towards Ryan to give him a kiss. 'Will you read me a story as well, Uncle Ryan——?'

'Only one story,' Heather interrupted. 'That's all we have time for tonight.'

'Oh!' Sarah's face fell. 'Well, will you read it for me?' She looked up at her father with wide, imploring eyes.

'I would consider it an honour,' he answered in a light, jesting voice, yet his eyes were serious and the hand that tweaked her chin was gentle to the point of tenderness. 'You run along and get into bed, and your mother can give me a call when you're ready.'

The child went quite happily after that.

Heather mused on the natural affinity there seemed to be between Sarah and her father as she bathed the little girl and got her ready for bed. The rapport between them had been almost instantaneous and it startled Heather.

'Are you going to get Uncle Ryan now?' the child asked impatiently as soon as the candy striped pyjamas were buttoned up.

Heather smiled. 'Yes, I'll get him now. You hop into bed.'

Heather was surprised to find Ryan in the kitchen stacking the dishwasher. 'You shouldn't be doing that!'

she told him with a frown.

'Why not?' He turned easily from his task. 'I ate the meal, didn't I?'

'Yes, but . . .' She trailed off in perplexity and then shrugged. 'Well, thank you anyway.'

'Any time,' he told her with a grin, bending to set the programme going on the machine. 'Is my presence required in the royal chamber?'

'It certainly is. Sarah is waiting with eager anticipation,' she told him with a smile. 'You know, you've scored quite a hit there.'

'She's scored a hit with me too,' he answered in a serious tone. 'She is a gorgeous child.' He walked towards Heather then, his eyes moved over her slim figure and the fine, delicate features of her face, a gleam of approval in their blue depths. 'But then she couldn't fail to be, could she?' he added in a deep, husky tone, making heat suffuse throughout Heather's body. She looked away from him, not knowing how to cope with this side of Ryan that was so disturbingly familiar from the past.

When he reached her side he tipped her chin gently up so that she was forced to look at him. A boyish grin curved his attractive mouth. 'Especially as she has such a good-looking father, eh, Heather?'

She had to laugh then at the outrageous way he had turned the compliment around. 'As long as she doesn't grow up with her father's modesty,' she answered, amusement glittering in her dark eyes as the tension inside her subsided.

'That wouldn't be such a bad thing,' he said with a smile as he placed a guiding hand at her back to turn her towards Sarah's room.

The child was sitting up in bed, her dark hair in

tumbled confusion around a little face that glowed with
animation. 'What took you so long?' she asked, eagerly
holding out a story-book towards her father.

'Patience, child,' he told her in a feigned stern tone,
taking the book from her. 'Which of these stories do you
want?' He leafed idly through the pages.

'The Three Little Pigs,' she told him immediately.

'Again?' Heather settled herself beside the child and
leaned back against the headboard. 'Don't you ever get
tired of that story?'

It seemed so strange having Ryan here, joining in
with their regular bedtime routine. If she closed her eyes
she could almost imagine that she was dreaming it all.
Ryan sitting on the edge of the bed, that gravel-deep,
attractive voice incongruent with the children's story.

She opened her eyes. Yes, he really was here. That
ruthless, unyielding businessman who had glared at her
across his desk only last week was sitting on the edge
of his daughter's bed, reading a story. Life threw the
most unexpected curves at you sometimes.

She allowed her eyes to linger on him as his attention
was on the book. The long sweep of his dark lashes that
she had always thought were wasted on a man. The vital
thickness of his dark hair that had the glorious hint of
fiery undertones. The handsomely rugged features and,
finally, the tantalising cleft in the firm chin.

He looked up suddenly, catching her blatantly staring
at him and, feeling extremely foolish, she looked
hurriedly away.

He closed the book with a snap. 'That's it, sweetheart.
The end of the story and time for you to get some sleep.'

'Oh, just one more,' Sarah implored.

'Maybe another night.' Ryan placed the book firmly
down on the bedside table. 'Now do I get a goodnight

kiss?'

The child nodded and held her arms up as Ryan leaned close.

For some strange reason Heather felt close to tears as she watched them, her heart aching for something that was hopelessly unattainable, something that she didn't even want to acknowledge.

'Your turn now, Mumma.' The child turned towards her and she cuddled the warm little body close against her.

'Now you be a good girl and go straight to sleep.' She pulled away reluctantly and tucked the covers around her before dropping another little kiss on her cheek.

'She's quite something else,' Ryan said when they stood outside the bedroom door.

Heather smiled in agreement and led the way through into the lounge. She noticed that Ryan had brought through the unfinished bottle of wine and their glasses.

'We may as well relax as we talk,' he said now as he poured them both a drink.

Heather sank down into the settee and stared into the flickering flames of the fire. 'So what exactly do you suggest we do?' Her voice was wary as she came straight to the point. 'How are we going to resolve this situation?'

He handed her glass to her and, instead of taking one of the chairs, sat down beside her. For a moment his eyes rested on her quietly, noting the anxiety that had returned to etch itself on her lovely features. 'Heather, I want you to understand that I'm not doing this to try and hurt you,' he said at last in a low voice. 'I know things have been strained between us and we've both said a lot of hurtful things to each other, but, as I said before, we are going to have to try and put all of that behind us and concentrate on Sarah.'

She nodded and took a sip of wine. Her hand trembled alarmingly on the stem of the glass and she tried desperately to steady it, not wanting him to see just how frightened she was by all of this. How much of Sarah's time would he want to occupy? What if he wanted to take her away from her for weeks on end?

He turned sideways on the settee, watching her intently. 'I lost my parents at a very young age,' he told her in a controlled, even tone. 'My childhood was spent being passed from one set of foster parents to another. I always swore that things would be different for my child, that he or she would have a secure home.'

She turned to meet his eyes then. She had known his parents were dead, but he had always glossed over the details and she had presumed it had happened when he was older. 'You never told me this before.'

He shrugged. 'To be honest, it's not something I care to remember. I only brought it up to try and make you understand why I feel so strongly that Sarah should have a good home life.'

'She has a good home life,' Heather retorted immediately.

'But she has no father. A child needs two parents, Heather,' he said firmly.

'I had two parents and, let me tell you, it didn't make me feel any more secure. They didn't love each other; they did nothing but fight. It was almost a relief when my father left.' Her voice shook with the shadows of remembrance.

For a moment there was a tense silence. 'I know your childhood was just as awful as mine,' he said softly. 'Don't you think that's all the more reason that we should try and give Sarah something better?'

'I suppose.' She bit down hard on her lip. 'But it's not going to make things any better if you take her away from me for weekends and holidays. She's only a baby, Ryan, and she needs me.'

'I know.' He leaned forward to put his untouched glass of wine down on the coffee-table. 'For the time being I will content myself with just getting to know my daughter. Bring her for visits to my home, trips out, that sort of thing. What I suggest is that you come too—that way Sarah will be relaxed and it will be more like a family outing for her.'

Heather closed her eyes. Admittedly his suggestion was much better than the dreadful nightmare that she had envisaged of Annabel and Ryan taking her child out, but she still felt a little tinge of apprehension. Would she be able to handle going out with Ryan and playing happy families? It sounded like dangerous territory to her.

'For God's sake, Heather, it needn't be that unpleasant. You might even enjoy it,' he grated harshly.

Her eyes flickered open to linger on his attractive face. That was what frightened her, she realised suddenly. That she might get to like it too much, and so might Sarah. Then where would that leave them?

'Well?' He interrupted her thoughts impatiently.

'I suppose that is the best solution.' She couldn't hide the reluctance in her voice.

'For now,' he said, his mouth tightening in a grim line.

'I don't suppose Annabel is going to be very pleased with this situation.' Her eyes glimmered with fear at the sudden unwanted thought. What if Ryan was just easing things to start with, thinking he could introduce Annabel to the child when she had grown used to him?

'To hell with Annabel,' he rasped. 'And don't for God's sake mention Craven's feelings on the subject because I don't want to hear them.'

'I wasn't going to.' She took another sip of her wine, feeling strangely calmer now. 'It's Sarah's birthday on Friday. Do you want to take things from there?'

He nodded. 'What plans have you made?'

'Nothing much. I'm taking the day off work and I was going to make a special tea and a birthday cake.'

'Well, leave all that. You can spend the day at my house and I'll get Mrs Marton to organise it.'

'You're going to take the whole day off?' Her eyes widened with surprise.

'Work has to take second priority to my daughter, Heather,' he told her quietly. 'I have missed her last three birthdays. I think I've got a lot of time to catch up on.' There was no reproach in his tone, but Heather knew it was there under the surface and she swallowed hard.

'Maybe I made a mistake not telling you I was pregnant, Ryan.' The words were stiff and difficult for her to say. 'But you had made it clear that you didn't want any commitments and . . . and we didn't love each other. I thought I was doing the right thing.' Why was she trying to justify herself to him? she wondered bleakly.

He watched her, his eyes deep blue and unfathomable. 'Let's just forget it, Heather. It's not going to help if we keep raking over it. We'll just have to try and put things right as best we can.'

She nodded, but for some strange reason felt close to tears. It suddenly seemed desperately important that he should understand, that he shouldn't think so badly of her. She put her glass down on the table and, as if that was his signal to leave, Ryan started to get to his feet.

'Well, time I was going,' he said lightly, picking up

his jacket from one of the chairs.

Heather got up, an inexplicable feeling of disappointment flaring through her body. 'I'll come down with you; I like to check that the main door is locked.'

He nodded and together they went out from the warmth and down the narrow stairway towards the street.

'Thanks for tonight, Heather.' He turned to her before opening the front door. 'It's meant a lot to me.'

For a moment they stood in the confined space of the hall, Heather looking up at him with wide dark eyes. His face was in shadow. She couldn't tell what he was thinking or feeling, but her body suddenly seemed alive with the most curious sensations. She felt like a girl on her first date, scared that the boy might kiss her, frightened that he might not. But Ryan was a man, not a boy, and this certainly was no date. She must be going quietly insane, she thought wildly.

Just as she thought Ryan was turning away from her, he bent his head down and his lips met hers. It was a kiss that was full of gentle sweetness and she felt dizzy with emotion when he finally pulled away.

'I'll pick you up around eleven on Friday.' Was it her imagination or did his voice sound as disturbed as she felt?

She nodded. Her heart seemed to be beating so loudly and erratically that she felt sure he must be able to hear it.

He turned then to open the door. They were both surprised by the weather outside. It was snowing quite heavily, large white flakes drifting across the darkness of the sky, covering the street and the cars in a silent blanket.

Heather's breath escaped in a shaky gasp. 'Are you driving back to Cheshire in this?'

He moved to look down at her. 'If I said I was, would you invite me to stay the night?' His voice was low and husky and it seemed to ignite the small flame that had been burning inside her into a blazing fire. In that moment she wanted to reach up and put her arms around his neck. She wanted him and it was a shock to realise just how much, but she knew it would be madness to give in to that need. Ryan didn't love her; she would just be an amusing diversion for him for the evening. Plus the fact that he was probably calculating that by getting closer to her he was one step nearer his daughter. Her eyes shadowed with that desolate thought.

'It's all right, Heather, don't look so panic-stricken.' His mouth twisted in a wry smile that was almost self-deprecating. 'I probably shouldn't have said that. Maybe I'm still a little punch-drunk from suddenly discovering I'm a father, or maybe I was forgetting for a moment that this isn't like old times.' He shrugged and turned up the collar on his coat. 'Anyway, I'll see you Friday.' Then he was gone, walking briskly towards his car, a tall, dark figure against a backdrop that was almost completely white.

She closed the door, her heart feeling as cold as that winter scene. No, this wasn't like old times, she thought grimly, and she should know better than to allow herself to weaken in any way towards him. Yet she had enjoyed his company this evening, and her heart had treasured seeing Sarah and her father together. Her mouth curved in a gentle smile as she remembered him sitting on the floor with her, and then later reading her that story. They were memories that she would always cherish.

She went slowly back upstairs and into the warmth of the apartment. The fire in the lounge was still burning brightly as she moved to make sure it was safe to leave before retiring to her room. For a moment she knelt beside it, staring into the flames. Ryan's strong, handsome face lingered disturbingly in her mind. The way he had laughed with Sarah during their meal, the way he had kissed her goodnight. She pressed the back of her hand against the softness of her lips, trying to close out the memory of that gentle caress, but it refused to go away, instead conjuring up ones that were even more disquieting. The velvet touch of Ryan's skin against hers as his body made love to her.

She swallowed hard on the tight knot of tears that rose in her throat What on earth was wrong with her? One poignant evening in Ryan's company and she was acting as if she was still in love with him. She drew in a shuddering breath as her senses suddenly relayed the truth to her. She *was* still in love with him!

Having him here, seeing him with Sarah had made her yearn for the impossible, had made her open her eyes to the fact that she still wanted him and needed him. Not just as Sarah's father, but as her lover. The knowledge hit her like a tidal wave, washing over her, engulfing her completely. When Ryan had kissed her she had wanted it to deepen into hungry demand. She had wanted . . . Hot colour scorched her face and she got up on to feet that seemed strangely unsteady. What was the point in loving him, and wanting him? Ryan didn't need her and he certainly didn't love her. He did however love his child—that one stark truth glared back at her and a million warning bells seemed to sound in her mind. She was going to have to tread very carefully. If Ryan ever discovered how she felt about him, he could very well use that vulnerability to his advantage in order to get closer to his daughter.

Heather went back to work the next day. She was feeling a little better and, knowing how the work would be piling up at the office, she decided to get back to it. Besides, keeping busy seemed to be the only way to keep her tortured mind from dwelling on Ryan.

Robert Craven was absolutely delighted to see her. 'Thank God!' he exclaimed dramatically when she walked in. 'I was just about to ring you up to see what on earth we were to do about tonight.'

Heather grinned ruefully. 'Well, as you can see, I'm feeling a lot better. What's happening tonight?'

Robert shook his head and waved her impatiently towards the seat at the other side of his desk. 'It's the opening night at Alan Aubery's new restaurant, remember?'

Heather grimaced. 'I'd forgotten all about that.'

'Well, don't look so gloomy about it. Aubery is one of the most distinguished restaurateurs in the country. Tonight's guest list will be strictly invitation only. You're damned lucky to have received one. Anybody who is anybody will be there.' He flicked the intercom through to his secretary, asking her to bring in Heather's invitation. 'Aubery was very impressed with the advertising campaign you handled for him. You could meet some important new business contacts tonight.'

Robert's private secretary came in and handed the gold-embossed envelope to him. He opened it briskly, skimming over its contents to refresh his memory. 'Yes, eight o'clock tonight. It's for you and me, but Richard will have to accompany you as I have something else on tonight.'

Heather nodded resignedly and took the envelope

from his outstretched hand. Every now and then she was required to attend functions like this on a business level. She didn't particularly enjoy them, but, as Robert had said, sometimes they were good for establishing new contacts and getting more business.

'By the way, we still haven't heard anything from Ryan Jameson. Give him a ring today and jog his memory, will you, Heather?'

The cool mention of Ryan's name made her nerves jump. She had forgotten to mention the contract to Ryan yesterday—in fact, it had gone clean out of her mind, something that she would have thought impossible a mere week ago. She nodded and went slowly back to her own office.

Once she was sitting behind her desk she eyed the telephone warily. She was apprehensive about ringing Ryan. Stupid, she knew, as this was a strictly business call, but somehow even the mere thought of talking to him sent shivers down her spine. She decided to put it off for a little while and started to do some other work instead. Later, after she had had time to gather herself together, she would contact him.

In the end the matter was taken out of her hands by Ryan's ringing her. Around midday Liz rang through on the intercom and told her that Mr Jameson was on the line and wished to speak to her.

Heather's heart started to beat a wild tattoo and she had to swallow down a sudden dryness in her throat as she reached for the receiver. 'Good morning, Ryan.' Somehow she managed to make her voice bright and informal.

'Good morning, Heather.' The deep, attractive voice held just a hint of amusement. 'I was surprised to learn that you had gone back to work when I rang your apartment this morning. How are you feeling?'

'Better, thank you.' Her tone sounded too brisk now. Why had he rung her at the apartment? she wondered uneasily. Was this a business call or something more personal? 'Actually I was just about to ring you myself. I was wondering if you still wanted us to go ahead with the advertising campaign?' She propelled the conversation straight on to business lines, cautiously avoiding anything else.

'Yes, don't worry about that. I'll come in and sign the contract some time today,' he replied in an offhand manner. 'What I really want to talk about is last night. I really enjoyed spending that time with you and Sarah.' His voice deepened on a husky, intimate tone now and it sent heat flaring through Heather's body in immediate response.

'We enjoyed your company as well,' she mumbled, feeling totally lost for words now.

'I was wondering if I could return the compliment by inviting you out for dinner this evening? Just you,' he added, with a low-pitched emphasis that made her heart dip wildly.

There was a silence for a moment while she did battle with wild emotion that wanted her to accept and forget about everything else, including her business dinner. Calm rationalism managed to fight its way to the surface and she shook her head. 'I'm sorry, Ryan, but I've got something on tonight. It's to do with work I——'

'It's all right, Heather, you don't need to explain,' he cut in abruptly. He didn't sound angry, but then he didn't sound too pleased either. 'Perhaps another time.'

'Perhaps.' Heather glared at the phone after she had replaced the receiver. She felt miserable and she was furious with herself for feeling like this, but she had desperately wanted to accept Ryan's invitation. If she hadn't already told Robert that she would attend this opening night she knew that she might have weakened and agreed.

'You're crazy,' she told herself disparagingly. It was going to be hard enough keeping herself coolly detached when she was in his company with Sarah. If she went out with him on her own she would be inviting heartache and trouble.

Resolutely she returned her attention to the work in front of her, trying to bury all thought of Ryan. Yet at the back of her mind a little spark of hope lingered that maybe she would see him this afternoon when he came in to sign the contract.

She went out at lunchtime and bought herself a new dress from a nearby boutique. It was a rich turquoise creation in a heavy silk material with an unusual design. It was a dress that emphasised her curvaceous yet slender figure, and gave her dark hair and eyes a mysterious exotic enchantment. She told herself that she was buying it because of the glittering up-market function she was to attend this evening, but the idea ran unchecked through her mind that if Ryan were to ask her out again, then maybe she would wear it for him.

By four o'clock she was beginning to wonder if Ryan had changed his mind about coming in today. Then, at four-thirty, Richard came in, a pleased smile lighting his handsome face.

'I thought you would like to know, we've just got the Redstar contract. Ryan Jameson has signed on the dotted line.'

'Is he here now?' Heather's eyes moved hopefully towards the door behind him.

'He's just left.'

'Oh!' Heather was conscious of disappointment and pain searing through her in equal measures. It was ridiculous to feel this hurt about something that should be good news. After all, the most important thing was that he had signed the contract; it was irrelevant that he had not wanted to see her while he was in. Yet it hurt—it hurt so much that she had a peculiar hollow feeling inside, a feeling that was suspiciously like the onset of tears.

'Well, you might at least look a little happy about it, Heather,' Richard remarked lightly, coming further into the room. 'This is wonderful news for the agency; it will give a terrific boost to our status.'

'Yes.' Heather leafed blindly through the papers in front of her and tried to summon a smile.

'It also means that we get to order champagne with our meal tonight.' Richard leaned forward on the desk. 'Father is feeling ecstatically generous.'

'Wonderful.' Heather managed to glance up at him. 'What time do you want to pick me up this evening?'

'I thought about half-seven, and with all this snow about I thought we should go by taxi.'

'Fine,' she murmured, not really caring how they got there.

'Heather?' The uncertain note in Richard's voice brought her head up sharply. 'I was just wondering if . . .if you would explain to Susan that our outing is just a business one. I asked her out the other day and I—er—wouldn't want her to think——'

'That's all right, Richard,' Heather interrupted with a smile. 'I'll explain to Susan. Maybe when we get back home you can have a drink with her. I don't want to be too late tonight anyway.'

Richard looked relieved and pleased by this and

nodded in agreement.

Later on that evening, as Heather stood in front of her bedroom mirror in the new turquoise dress, she was strongly wishing that Richard was taking Susan. She just wasn't in the mood for going anywhere.

Why had Ryan called to ask her out? she wondered for the hundredth time. Had it simply been a case of wanting to repay her for last night's meal? Probably, she thought dully. It couldn't have meant anything deeper—not when he hadn't even bothered to look in on her when he was at the offices today.

There was a tap on the door and Susan came in. 'Wow!' Her eyes lit up at the picture her boss presented. 'You look fabulous. Like one of those exotic James Bond girls.'

Heather had to laugh at that. 'Thank you. Has 007 arrived yet?'

'Yes, he's in the hall.' Susan grinned. 'Though, much as I like Richard, I think the man who was here with you the other day fits that description more aptly.'

Heather's mouth tightened. Why was it that the merest reference to Ryan could make her heartbeats increase dramatically? she wondered angrily.

It had started to snow again by the time they reached the restaurant. Heather was glad of the white cashmere coat as she stepped out of the taxi and into the cold.

'Better watch your step,' Richard warned as he got out beside her. Then, as she almost slipped on the icy surface of the pavement, he placed a steadying arm around her waist.

'It wasn't very sensible of me to wear these high heels, was it?' Heather grimaced.

'Well, it's only a couple of steps to the restaurant,' Richard told her with smiling good humour.

Heather's head was down as she concentrated on her footsteps over the treacherous ground, therefore she didn't notice the other couple who just reached the restaurant door before them until Richard spoke to them.

'Well, hello there, Mr Jameson. This is a surprise.'

Heather's head jerked up, her eyes clashing immediately with Ryan's hard blue gaze.

'Yes, isn't it?' he grated harshly. His eyes moved from Heather's face to the arm that Richard had protectively kept around her waist. 'You finished work earlier than you had planned, then, Heather?'

She swallowed and was about to explain that their visit to the restaurant was connected with work when her eyes moved to the woman at his side.

Annabel was wearing a silver-fox fur coat, her blonde hair gleaming in the light that streamed out behind her from the old coaching lamps that lit the entrance to the building. Why on earth should she bother to explain? she suddenly thought angrily. Ryan obviously wouldn't be making any explanations as to why he was here with Annabel. So she nodded, switching her attention defiantly back to Ryan.

'Well, it's very pleasant that we should all meet up like this,' he said in a light vein, and stood to one side to allow the two women to precede them into the restaurant. For all his charm and good manners, Heather couldn't help but think there was something vaguely menacing about his manner. He was somehow too suave, too polite.

Alan Aubery's restaurants lived up to the glossy image that Heather's advertising campaign had helped to create: stylishly expensive, with an intimate, romantic ambience. A log fire filled the huge stone fireplace at one end of the room, sending flickering light out over the dance-floor, and the tables were set discreetly apart. Candle-light and the subdued glow from Tiffany lights gleamed on the polished silver settings on each table.

A waiter came quickly towards them to take their coats. As Heather slipped out of hers she noticed the way Ryan's eyes lingered on her, taking in every curve of her body in the turquoise silk. Heat flooded through her veins at that appreciative male scrutiny and she turned away from him, embarrassed and confused. She hoped to goodness that Ryan and Annabel would disappear to their table as soon as possible. She didn't think she could stand the strain of having them around for too long.

The waiter led them through into the bar area where most of the guests seemed to have converged to sip champagne and toast Alan's new restaurant. Heather could see him circulating among them, looking resplendent in a white dinner-jacket. He spotted them immediately and came hurrying across.

'Darling, lovely to see you again.' He kissed Heather warmly on each cheek. 'You look radiant, absolutely radiant.'

His attention suddenly transferred itself to Ryan. 'Thrilled you could make it, Mr. Jameson.' He frowned for a moment as he seemed to notice that the four of them had arrived at the same time. 'Are you all together, Mr Jameson? Would you like a table for four?'

'If that wouldn't be a problem,' Ryan answered smoothly.

'Of course not, no problem at all.' As Alan disappeared to see to changing his seating arrangements, Heather turned furious eyes up at Ryan.

He might at least have consulted them before rearranging their evening!

He met her gaze with eyes that glittered with amusement. 'That does meet with your approval, doesn't it, Heather?'

Her mouth tightened into a firm angry line. He knew damn well that it did not, yet she could hardly make a fuss in front of everyone, so she merely shrugged her shoulders nonchalantly.

One glance in Annabel's direction told her that she on the other hand would not have been so guarded in her reply if he had asked her. She looked absolutely enraged. The other woman looked over towards her just then and for a moment there was open animosity in her cold blue eyes.

'Ryan has been telling me all about your little girl.' Annabel's topic of conversation made Heather's eyebrows rise warily. 'How old is she, three?'

'Four on Friday.' Heather was relieved when the waiter arrived with their champagne, hoping that the subject would now be dropped. Discussing her child with this woman made her feel most uneasy.

'Having a child of that age must be a terrible hindrance to your career,' Annabel carried on, unperturbed by the waiter's presence.

'Not really,' Heather murmured as she took the delicate champagne flute offered to her.

'Heather is one of those remarkable women who are able to balance motherhood with their careers and excel at both of them,' Ryan intervened gently.

The unexpected praise from him sent a rosy warmth into the paleness of her skin. Ryan was not the type of man to utter meaningless compliments, so his approval meant a lot to Heather.

'Even so,' Annabel continued sharply, 'it must be difficult—especially when you're a single parent.'

The glow of happiness died a very quick death inside Heather. Just how much of her business had Ryan been discussing with this woman? How much did she know? Her fingers tightened angrily around the stem of her glass. It made her feel positively sick to think of them talking about her at all.

'I'm afraid that I don't particularly care for children at all.' Annabel placed one hand down on to the gold-sequined dress, emphasising the exquisite slender curves of her body. 'Apart from everything else, they ruin your figure.' She allowed her eyes to rest for just a second too long on Heather's trim figure, managing to make her feel as if she were hideously out of shape.

'Now I can't agree with you there, Annabel,' Richard put in suddenly. 'I mean, look at Heather.' He placed a light, jovial arm around her waist. 'She has a stunning figure. There is absolutely no reason why a woman should lose her looks just because she's become a mother. In fact, in a lot of cases it adds a new dimension to a woman's beauty.'

Heather gave him a small, grateful smile and was quite thankful for the way his arm lingered at her side. This evening was turning into a nightmare. Ryan's eyes had locked on them in a way that was totally unnerving.

Alan arrived back at that moment and told them their table was ready, and it was with a feeling of reprieve that Heather turned to follow him through to the dining-room.

Heather wasn't able to do full justice to the spectacular culinary delights of the evening. She was painfully aware of Ryan sitting across the table from her. He seemed to be watching her every move, his eyes lingering on the porcelain smoothness of her complexion and the dark expressive eyes that fought very hard not to meet his gaze. She focused all her attention on Richard, talking to him almost exclusively. This seemed to please Annabel, but Heather could tell that for some reason it was infuriating Ryan.

When the coffee and liqueurs were served, Ryan suddenly reached out a hand and captured Heather's. 'How about a dance?' he asked her abruptly.

She glanced at the small dance-floor where a few couples were swaying to the intimate romantic tones of a piano, and was about to refuse when he practically yanked her to her feet. 'Excuse us, won't you?' he said politely to the other two before leading her firmly away.

'What the hell do you think you are playing at?' she asked breathlessly as he pulled her forcibly into his arms.

'I was about to ask you the same thing,' he snapped back. 'You've been positively drooling over that Craven idiot all evening.'

'Don't be ridiculous.' She tried to hold herself as far away as possible from his body. 'Besides, that idiot as you call him happens to be my date for the evening.'

Ryan's mouth tightened angrily. 'Well, I suggest that you get rid of him very quickly when you leave here, my darling, because you and I have things to discuss.' His voice was heavy and the endearment faintly ominous.

'We had our discussion last night.' Heather stared up at him in bewilderment. His face was enigmatic, yet those blue eyes glittered with a strange intentness. He seemed to have lost the calm reason that he had possessed yesterday when he had visited her apartment.

'Get rid of him, Heather,' he warned. 'Or I won't be

answerable for the consequences.'

'You have no right to dictate to me like this.' Her voice shook, but it was as much from fear as anger. 'I've given in to your stipulations on seeing your daughter, but I am not your possession, Ryan. You cannot tell me who I can and cannot see. Anyway, you've got a damn nerve, considering that you're here with Annabel.'

'Forget about Annabel,' he grated.

'That is a little difficult when her eyes are stabbing into my back,' she answered with a disdainful toss of her head.

The music ended just then and Ryan released her. 'Are you going to do as you're told?' he demanded bluntly.

Heather's lips tightened furiously. How dared he adopt this high-handed, proprietary attitude. 'Go to hell,' she muttered fiercely before swinging away towards their table.

She didn't return to her seat, but stood next to it as she looked over towards Richard. 'I hate to break up the party,' her tongue tripped lightly over such a lie, 'but, Richard, would you mind if we went home now——?'

Ryan also made no move to sit down, and she was startled to find that as she finished speaking his hand curved around her small waist. 'Heather's not feeling very well,' he cut in briskly. 'And as I have the car outside I have offered to take her home.'

Furious at this outrageous lie, Heather tried to shrug him away from her. But he was holding her so tightly that it was impossible to move without causing a scene.

Richard started to rise from his seat and Ryan quickly waved him down. 'No, don't let this ruin the evening for you and Annabel. I know that Alan has some cabaret entertainment lined up for later on, and it would be a shame for us all to miss it.' Heather bit down furiously at the smooth, effortless way that he was manipulating everyone.

Richard sat back down again, looking less than pleased with this turn of events, but not daring to voice any objections. 'Very well, Mr Jameson, if that's what you want,' he muttered weakly, making Heather cringe.

'Good man, and perhaps you would see Annabel back to her hotel later?' He turned a charming smile down on the other woman, but it didn't quite manage to melt the fury that was building up in her blue eyes. 'Sorry about this, honey, but maybe all is not lost. Richard knows all about the advertising campaign that I was talking about earlier, so perhaps he will fill you in on a few details.'

Without waiting for anyone to say anything else, he steered Heather very firmly away towards the door.

'How dare you do this?' Heather muttered in a tight, furious voice as they stood and waited for the waiter to fetch their coats.

'I dare to do anything I damn well please,' he answered in a low, controlled voice.

Had Heather not disliked scenes, she would have snatched her coat from the waiter and stormed out; as it was, she waited and allowed him to help her on with it, telling herself that once they got outside she would make her feelings very clear, and there was no way that she was going anywhere with Ryan.

Alan Aubery detained them by the door, asking them anxiously if everything was all right with their meal.

'Perfect,' Ryan assured him in a deep, steady voice. 'Sorry we have to dash off so early, but Heather isn't feeling very well.'

'Oh, dear.' There was concern in Alan's kind face and Heather's blood boiled at the insidious position Ryan had placed her in. 'And I was hoping that perhaps later we could discuss some ideas for a further advertising campaign.'

Heather opened her mouth to answer him, but Ryan wasn't taking any chances and quickly cut in, 'Perhaps another time,' as he placed a hand under her elbow to move her firmly away.

The cold air was a shock to Heather's flushed body as they stepped out of the warmth of the restaurant. It was snowing very heavily and an icy wind was slanting the white flakes into a thick carpet on the deserted street.

Once the door had closed behind them Heather tore her arm from him and started to walk hurriedly away in the opposite direction without saying a word. She kept her head down against the weather, concentrating on her steps while her mind reeled with fury at Ryan.

'Where the hell do you think you are going?' He caught up with her before she had got very far.

'As far away from you as it is possible to get,' she answered through clenched teeth, without lifting her head.

'Don't be ridiculous.' The touch of his hand on her sleeve was all it took to unleash the turbulence inside her.

She swung around, her dark eyes bright with wild, livid light. 'How dare you?' She practically spat the words at him. 'How dare you treat me like one of your damned possessions? I don't belong to you and you have no right to dictate to me, especially with that—that woman at your side.'

'I'm sorry.' The quietly spoken apology took her by complete surprise, making all the harsh, enraged words die a very quick death.

She stared up at him in perplexity. An aura of grim

resolve seemed to circle him as he met her eyes. 'I'm sorry if I've upset you, but not for bringing you away from Craven.'

There was silence as they just continued to stand there looking at each other. Ryan looked powerfully forbidding in the dark, heavy overcoat, the snow slanting across his broad figure, a few white flakes daring to linger in the crisp thickness of his dark hair. He looked austere and determined, like a dark angel of death against a background of eerie whiteness. 'Seeing you with Craven made me realise just how much I despise the thought of you with another man.'

Because of Sarah, Heather thought bleakly. She jammed her hands into her coat pocket, clenching them into tight fists. She couldn't blame him for feeling like that; she had the same feeling of jealousy every time she thought that Annabel might have any involvement in her child's life. Only her feelings of resentment stemmed from much deeper emotions than his. She wasn't just feeling possessive over her child, she was in love with him.

'Marry me, Heather.'

For a moment she thought she had misheard the softly spoken words. The breeze seemed to snatch them away from him, carrying them away into the cold night air.

'I can offer you a much better life than Craven could possibly hope to.'

Heather held his steady gaze. 'You mean, I suppose, that you can give me greater material wealth?'

He nodded, cold silver light entering his blue eyes.

'But that isn't what I want, Ryan,' she stated thickly. 'If financial security was all I wanted I would have stuck around four and a half years ago, because I never believed for one minute that you had any money problems.'

For a moment he looked lost and bewildered—two emotions totally alien to Ryan Jameson. Heather swallowed down on a hard knot of tears that wanted to fight its way to the surface. He had been so certain in his judgement of her, had thought he'd known exactly what motivated her, that all he had to do was offer his wealth and she would be his.

'So what do you want, then?' Ryan asked huskily, his eyes searching the unhappiness of her pale face.

'How about love?' she asked softly.

A pulse beat at the side of his strong jaw and his eyes were bleak. 'Given time, it could grow. We have the love of our child in common; we can take it from there.'

CHAPTER NINE

SARAH kept dashing backwards and forwards from the window.

'Uncle Ryan is going to come, Mumma, isn't he?' she asked for the hundredth time in a highly excited little voice.

'Yes, darling, any minute now,' Heather answered absently. She put down the silver-backed hairbrush and studied her reflection in the dressing-table mirror—the heavy tumble of blue-black hair in a shimmering cloud around the porcelain paleness of her oval face. There were faint shadows beneath her wide eyes that she had tried unsuccessfully to hide. She looked tired, which was hardly surprising considering she had hardly slept at all these last few nights since Ryan's proposal.

Just thinking about that made her heart twist painfully. His offer of marriage had been so harsh and bleak, as cold as the weather that had swirled around them.

When she had been expecting Sarah, she had sometimes allowed herself to fantasise that Ryan would find her and ask her to marry him. The scene she had imagined had always been the same. He had held her tenderly in his arms and had said, 'I love you, Heather, and I need you.' A bitter smile tugged at her lips and she closed her eyes. Dream on, she told herself scathingly. What a romantic fool you are.

Ryan's proposal the other night was cruel reality. He had made no attempt to disguise his reason for asking her. He wanted his child, it was as simple as that. No tender words or feelings, no attempt even to touch her. He had driven her home in cold, stony silence and his only parting words had been a grim, 'Think it over.' As if they were discussing some business merger. Come to think of it, that was probably what it was to him. He had certainly left her no room to hope that he might care for her.

The awful thing was that she wanted so desperately to accept, and if he had offered her one tiny shred of hope she would have used it to feed that yearning need inside her. She wanted to hide from reality and follow the longing inside her heart, and that was a dangerous path to tread.

'Here he is, here he is!' Sarah scampered away from the window to come and tug at her mother's sleeve. 'Come and open the door, Mumma. Uncle Ryan is here.'

From somewhere Heather managed to summon a smile for the child as she got slowly and reluctantly to her feet.

The sound of the doorbell made her heart pound with unmerciful hard, painful strokes, and she moved stiffly to answer it.

As usual that unbidden surge of awareness flooded through her at the sight of him. He was wearing a pair of tight-fitting faded blue jeans and a thick navy Aran sweater, and he looked devastatingly handsome in the casual attire: all man, powerful, rugged, sensual man.

The blue eyes swept quickly over her in an all-encompassing appraisal, from the tip of her gleaming hair down over the fitted cream wool top and full skirt to the soft brown leather boots. It was impossible to decipher exactly what was going on in his mind behind that masculine gleam of approval. When his glance moved to Sarah, however, it was very easy to read his feelings.

Tenderness softened the harsh attractive planes of his

face as he bent to swing her up into his arms. 'Happy birthday, honey.'

Sarah curled her arms around his neck, a smile of pure happiness curving her lips and lighting up her face. 'Are we really going to your house, Uncle Ryan?'

'You sure are, and I've got a big surprise waiting for you,' he answered easily before putting the little girl gently down.

'Gosh! What is it?' Sarah demanded at once.

'Well, if I told you it wouldn't be a surprise.' Ryan grinned. 'You'll have to wait and see.' He turned towards Heather and for a moment the warmth in his expression lingered. 'Are you ready to go?'

'Yes, I'll just get Sarah's coat.' She turned away from him, hiding her disquiet behind a feigned practical manner.

How could she ever have imagined that Ryan would be unable to feel love for his daughter? she wondered suddenly, a cold, bleak feeling settling around her heart. That assumption seemed nonsensical now, and dreadfully arrogant and selfish. Just because he was unable to love her, it didn't mean that he was incapable of loving. Seeing Sarah with her father made Heather realise just how wrong she had been. Her decision had denied Ryan the right to know his daughter, and had robbed Sarah of her father. A father whom she obviously adored.

She watched Ryan kneel to button up Sarah's coat with a tight feeling in her throat. Four years ago she had been certain that she had acted for all the right reasons. She hadn't wanted Ryan to feel trapped and obliged to them, so she had taken all the responsibility on to her own shoulders and had made decisions that she had had no right to make on her own. She had made a terrible and unforgivable mistake.

It was cold outside. The roads had been cleared of snow now, but the pavements were still treacherous and Ryan carried Sarah while keeping one firm hand on Heather's arm.

'I've brought the Range Rover today. Conditions on the country roads aren't as good as they are in the city,' Ryan explained as he opened the passenger door for Heather and then placed Sarah in the back, fastening the seatbelt securely around her.

'We were wondering if you would be able to come,' Heather remarked as he settled himself beside her.

He flung a disdainful harsh glance in her direction. 'Sorry to disappoint you, but it would take more than a couple of inches of snow to keep me away.'

She flushed, her expression becoming contrite. 'I didn't mean it like that,' she told him gruffly. 'Sarah would have been very disappointed if you hadn't arrived. She's really been looking forward to spending the day with you.'

'Well, at least that makes one of you.' He started up the car, his expression one of grim thoughtfulness.

Heather swallowed and looked away from him. He would have been very shocked if he knew how she also had been longing for his arrival. She would have given anything to have been able to go into his arms as Sarah had done, unreservedly, with no fear of rejection.

Heather was thankful for Sarah's happy chatter as they drove; it helped to break the tension that hung between Ryan and her. Would he bring up the subject of marriage again? she wondered. Or was he already regretting the impetuous offer? Marriage to a woman he despised was a high price to pay for his daughter. If he did mention it, what would she say?

When they arrived at Ryan's home he didn't take them inside immediately. Instead he suggested that they go and find Sarah's birthday surprise.

'Where is it, Uncle Ryan?' Sarah looked up at him with wide shining eyes. She looked adorable in the bright red little trouser-suit, a red woollen hat tilted sideways over her gleaming dark hair. 'Is it hiding somewhere outside?'

'You could say that.' Ryan smiled teasingly. 'Why don't you run over there and have a look?' He pointed towards the side of the house and at once the child turned to do as he asked. Her little legs scrunched over the crisp white snow in the colourful red boots.

'What have you bought her?' Heather asked him curiously, as they followed at a more sedate pace.

'I told you, it's a surprise,' he grinned, an infuriating light in his blue eyes as he watched the gleam of impatience cross the lovely lines of her face. 'Motherhood suits you, do you know that, Heather?' he told her suddenly. 'You're even more beautiful now than when I first met you.'

She flushed a bright, brilliant red at the unexpected compliment, turning startled eyes on him.

He smiled. 'And I'm able to make you blush with the same amazing ease as I was back then. I must still have the ability to stir up some feeling, awaken some of your senses.'

All of them, she thought, a strange melting sensation invading her body as he reached out an arm to pull her close.

'Did you love him?' The sudden granite-hard question jerked her out of her reverie.

'Love whom?' She frowned.

'Edwards.' His voice was bleak. 'Did you marry him

out of love?'

Heather drew in a deep, trembling breath. She should tell him the truth; she owed him at least that much. Maybe if she was honest, told him everything . . .?

He let her go abruptly. 'It's all right, Heather, you needn't answer. I don't even know what made me ask.' His rough tone jarred through her body, rubbing her already sensitive nerves raw.

She watched him striding away from her towards his daughter, tears blurring his dark figure.

She followed them slowly, wiping a cold, shaking hand surreptitiously over her eyes in case they might notice her distress.

Sarah's excited cries rang out clearly in the cold, still air as father and daughter turned the corner into the courtyard behind the house. Frowning, Heather moved with more speed to catch up with them.

Sarah was jumping up and down. 'Look at my birthday present, Mumma, just look!'

Heather was looking, her eyes widening in disbelief as they fell on the small grey Shetland pony with a big red ribbon around its neck.

'First rule, no sudden movement or loud noises,' Ryan told his daughter gently as he picked her up. 'You don't want to frighten him, do you?'

Sarah shook her head. 'Can I ride him now, Uncle Ryan?' she asked in a loud stage whisper.

He nodded and placed her gently on the leather saddle, adjusting the stirrups to her little feet with deft movements.

'Look at me, Mumma, look at me!' Sarah glanced over at Heather, an expression of pride and rapture on her face.

'You look wonderful, darling.' Heather smiled gently.

She watched while Ryan started to walk the pony very slowly, keeping a cautious hand around the child's back.

He flicked a glance at her as they passed. 'You may as well go inside, Heather. There's no point in your catching cold just standing there.'

Heather swallowed down the hurt and resentment at being dismissed so abruptly. He might as well have said, Go home, we don't need you.

Heather let herself into the house by the back door and went through to the kitchen. Mrs Marton was busy preparing Sarah's birthday tea, which, judging by the mouth-watering dishes spread out along the worktops, was going to be quite a feast.

'Hello, Mrs Edwards.' The housekeeper turned towards her, a welcoming smile on her face. 'How are you now?'

'A lot better, thank you.' Heather placed a rueful hand towards the slight graze on her forehead. 'I'm sorry about all the fuss I caused last Saturday.'

'It wasn't your fault.' Mrs Marton shook her head. 'When Mr Jameson told me that there was something wrong with that car I felt just awful; I would never have let you take it if I had known.'

'No, of course not,' Heather said immediately, and then grinned. 'Anyway, I did put a bit of pressure on you.'

'You looked very distressed.' Mrs Marton opened the refrigerator and took out some double cream, before looking over at Heather with a smile. 'Mr Jameson said that when you look at him like that he has trouble denying you something too.'

'Did he?' Heather's eyebrows shot up and a little thrill ran through her body, before she realised suddenly that Ryan had probably said that to make his housekeeper feel better about the incident. She let her breath out in a sigh and watched the other woman as she carried on working. 'You shouldn't be going to all this trouble,' she told her softly.

'Oh, it's no trouble—I'm enjoying it. It's a long time since I prepared a child's birthday party.'

'Well, let me do something to help.' Heather waved the woman's objection away. 'Honestly, I really would like to,' she told her truthfully. It would be a relief just to keep busy and stop herself dwelling on Ryan.

Time seemed to fly after that. Ryan and Sarah came into the kitchen just as Heather was placing the candles on the magnificent birthday cake.

'Did you see me riding Oliver, Mumma? Did you?' The child raced towards her, eyes alive with excitement, her face glowing from the fresh air.

'Yes, I saw you.' Heather smiled, bending down to remove her coat and hat. 'Is that what you are calling him—Oliver?'

Sarah nodded and Heather turned laughing eyes up towards Ryan. 'I don't know where she gets these names from. I gave her a doll for her birthday and she has insisted on calling her Henry!'

'It's short for Henrietta,' Sara inserted in a grave little voice, making her father laugh.

'Obviously a child of high intelligence,' he drawled. 'It has started to snow again out there, very heavily as well,' he continued. 'I hope it's not going to keep this up or we might have difficulty getting back to Manchester.'

The tinge of alarm that comment stirred up continued to grow as the afternoon progressed. The snow was falling with driving force, drifting across the window like a great white curtain. The sky was so heavy and white that it merged with the landscape, creating a silver world that looked bleak and unearthly. It was the type of day that made you glad to be inside, safe and warm beside a fire, away from the wild forces of nature.

Ryan caught her watching it as they sat in the lounge after tea. 'I'm not going to even attempt to take you back home in this,' he told her suddenly. 'You and Sarah are going to have to spend the night here.'

Heather's gaze swivelled quickly to meet his. 'But we can't, I haven't brought——'

'I'm sure you will survive for once without your night things,' he cut in, correctly reading her thought. 'Besides, if I remember correctly you never used to wear a nightdress,' he went on, a gleam of devilment in his blue eyes. 'Well, not after the first night in my bed.'

She coloured furiously at his words and the memories they conjured up. She remembered how shy she had been when she had first moved in with him.

On their first night together she had chosen to wear a Victorian-type nightdress which covered her from head to toe. When she had walked back through to the bedroom he had already been sitting up in the bed, his bronzed torso naked and gleaming in the lamp light, the covers low enough down on his hips to tell her that he wore nothing beneath them. His eyes had raked over her attire, a gentle smile curving his lips. 'That,' he had said, 'will have to go.' Then he had proceeded to get out of the bed with such a purposeful look about him that she had instinctively backed away. Once he had caught her, however, her fear had melted to excitement, passion and pure happiness.

Flustered, she looked away from him. 'I really can't remember,' she lied unsteadily.

His face darkened. 'Can't remember, or don't want to?'

'Both.' She stood up abruptly, holding out her hand towards Sarah. 'Come on, sweetheart. We're staying at Uncle Ryan's house tonight, and it's time to go to bed.'

'Running away, Heather?' One dark eyebrow rose and there was an underlying note of anger in his voice.

'Probably.' She sounded tired suddenly, and she felt exhausted. She watched Sarah run towards her father, climbing up on to his knee and lifting her face for his goodnight kiss, and she swallowed on the lump of weak emotion forming in her throat.

'Are you going to come up and read me a story?' Sarah asked as she slipped back down.

He shook his head. 'Not tonight, honey.' He looked over at Heather. 'I don't suppose you're coming back down again?'

She shook her head. 'Which room can we have?'

He got up, crossing the room towards the drinks cabinet to pour himself a generous measure of whisky. 'You can have the first on the left at the top of the stairs, and Sarah can have the one next to it.' He slanted an oblique look in her direction as she moved to the door. 'See you later.'

'See you in the morning,' she corrected him with a frown.

When Heather opened the first door that he had indicated upstairs she came to an abrupt halt. This was no guest room, it was Ryan's own bedroom. It had Ryan's character stamped all over it—an intensely masculine room in rich shades of brown, russet silk covers on the enormous double bed, a silver framed photograph of someone on the table next to it, one of his expensive suits on a hanger next to the built-in wardrobes.

'I think this is Uncle Ryan's idea of a joke,' Heather

murmured to Sarah, backing quickly out again.

'Why?' Sarah looked up at her with wide, puzzled eyes.

'Because this is not our room,' Heather answered firmly. She was relieved to find that the one next door contained a double bed, with a small annex adjoining it which had a single bed suitable for Sarah.

Very funny, Ryan, she thought grimly as she undressed the child ready for bed. She had a good mind to go downstairs and tell him exactly what she thought of his sick joke.

That idea had faded, however, by the time Sarah was tucked up and drifting off to sleep. What was the point? she thought grimly. She went back into her own room and started to undress down to her silk lingerie.

It was as she was slipping beneath the cool covers of her bed that she remembered the silver photo beside his bed. Who was in that frame? she wondered suddenly. She wished now that she had gone further in to look at it. Then, disgusted with herself, she turned over, burying her head in her pillows. It would be Annabel's photograph, of course; who else would have pride of place next to his bed?

She tossed and turned for a long time, her mind filled with disturbing thoughts and images of Ryan. He had made no reference today about his proposal; she could only assume that it had been a wild and now-regretted impulse. He was probably wondering now how he could make things right for him and Annabel.

At some point she must have dozed off into a deep and troubled sleep, for the next thing she was conscious of was a man's voice cutting through her dreams.

She sat up, pushing the dark flow of tumbled long hair out of her eyes as she tried to focus on the dark shadow in her doorway.

'Heather, are you awake?' It was Ryan's voice, deep and velvety in the silence of the night, making her wonder if she was still asleep and dreaming.

'Heather, Sarah has been crying for you.' At the same time as he spoke she heard the whimper from the child in the adjoining room. Instinctively she flung back the bed clothes, rubbing the sleep from her eyes as she walked towards the connecting door. In her dreamlike state she was unaware that all she wore was the silk and lace camisole and matching briefs, and that Ryan's eyes were moving over her long, bare legs and curving body in open appraisal.

'What is it, darling?' Heather sat on the edge of the child's bed and put her arms around the little girl.

'Where am I?' The child opened wide, tear-filled eyes for a moment, but she sounded as if she were still asleep.

'You're at Uncle Ryan's house, remember?' She cradled the child gently.

'Oh, yes.' Her eyelashes fluttered closed and a smile curved the rosebud mouth. 'I love Uncle Ryan,' she murmured softly as sleep overtook her again.

Heather wiped the tears from the little girl's cheeks, placing her tenderly back against the pillows. For a moment she just stared down at the child, a feeling of ineffable sadness washing through her.

'Heather.' Ryan's hand touched the bare satin skin of her shoulder, startling her out of her reverie. 'Come back to bed, she's fast asleep.'

'Yes.' She stared up at him, the intimacy of the words striking a chord deep inside her.

'Come on then, before you catch cold.' His voice was low and gentle, yet there was nothing gentle about the way his eyes were sweeping over her in the half-light.

That look made her acutely conscious of her undress, the immodest silk and lace of her lingerie that hid very little of her shapely figure. She got unsteadily to her feet, walking self-consciously in front of him back towards her own bed.

She flicked a glance at him as she climbed in beneath the covers. He was still fully dressed and obviously hadn't gone to bed yet. 'What time is it?'

He moved towards the window, pulling back the curtains so that silver moonlight flooded the room. 'Three,' he answered, glancing at his watch as he moved back to her and, much to Heather's discomposure, sat on the edge of the bed beside her.

'Why aren't you in bed?' She struggled to sit up and he reached past her to arrange her pillows. The aroma of his cologne lingered softly around her as he moved back, a wry smile curving his lips.

'Is that an invitation?'

'No, it is not.' She glanced up at him sharply. 'And while we're on the subject, why did you direct me into your bedroom this evening?'

'Because I wanted you in my bed, why else?' His voice had a husky edge to it that made her heartbeats increase dramatically. 'That's where you belong, Heather.'

'Don't be ridiculous.' She looked away from him, but he caught her chin in one firm hand, forcing her to meet his gaze.

Her body quivered at the blaze that she encountered in those smoky blue eyes. 'You belong to me, Heather, and I want you back. I want what's mine.'

His mouth came down on hers with no warning. One minute he was talking in a hard, biting voice, the next his arms were pulling her towards him in a steel-like embrace, his lips forcing hers apart in a kiss that was filled with a terrible hunger.

Shock held her passive in those arms for a moment, then, as his lips softened and roved teasingly around the smooth oval of her face, across her forehead, over her eyelids as they fluttered closed and down over her cheeks, she gave a low groan of protest. As she turned her head, yearning for the touch of his lips against hers again, her mouth sought and then found his, and suddenly the storm of emotion that had been building up inside her exploded.

'Ryan, I want . . .' Her voice was husky and incoherent with the force of her need for him, and she brought slender arms up and around his shoulders, allowing her hands to twine into the thickness of his dark hair.

She felt him shudder and he moved his head downwards, tasting the smooth tenderness of her shoulder. His hand stroked her body, spanning her waist through the silk of her lingerie before moving upwards to the lace that cupped her breasts.

'God, you are beautiful.' His voice was rough with emotion, his hand caressing, stroking so that fire licked through her at a frightening speed.

He brought one hand up to gently ease her back against the pillows, and for a moment he sat looking down at her. His hand still caressed her throbbing breast and a small triumphant smile lit his features as he noted her response to him. Her hair was a glossy blue-black cloud against the pillows, her lovely eyes dark with need as she stared up at him, her kiss-swollen lips parted.

'Tell me you want me,' he demanded softly. 'Put me out of my misery and let me hear you say it.'

'I want you.' Her voice was a husky whisper in the silence that surrounded them. 'I've always wanted you.'

CHAPTER TEN

WHEN Heather surfaced from sleep she felt lazily relaxed, and she lay for a moment, drifting between sleep and wakefulness, wondering why her body felt so wonderful. She stretched languidly and turned, coming face to face with Ryan.

A slow, teasing smile curved his lips as he noted the expression on her face. 'You surely hadn't forgotten about me, had you?' He reached out a hand to pull her naked body close in against his. 'Mmm.' He nuzzled his face into the soft, vulnerable curve of her neck. 'I thought you were never going to wake up.' His mouth moved upwards in a series of slow, drugging kisses until he reached her mouth.

His skin was slightly abrasive this morning against the smooth satin of hers, and it stirred up a wanton eagerness inside her that shocked and thrilled her at the same time.

Memories from the night before flooded through her mind. Words whispered in the silver darkness of the night. Hands and lips caressing and tormenting her body to unbearable heights of passion and pleasure. Ryan's hard, powerful body possessing her again and again.

She looked up at him with wide, uncertain eyes, and a smile curved his firm mouth. 'Don't look at me like that,' he admonished lightly, raining small kisses down over her upturned face.

A multitude of delicious sensations teemed inside her at his touch. 'Like what?' She smiled.

'As if I've left some part of your anatomy unloved,' he grinned.

'I think you've more or less covered every part of my anatomy,' she assured him, a shy warm colour stealing up under her skin.

His laugh was a low, growling sound in his throat as he rolled over her and gazed down, warmth and tenderness in his eyes. 'It's been a long time since we lay like this together.' His voice was suddenly serious. 'I'd almost forgotten how beautiful it is.'

She nodded, reaching up to trace a gentle finger down the side of his strong jawline until it reached the cleft in his chin. How could she ever have imagined that she could live without him? she wondered achingly.

As the pearl-grey light of dawn stole softly over the room Ryan made love to her again, this time without the wild urgency of the previous night. His mouth gentled hers, coaxing her body, making her gasp and tremble, electrifying every nerve-ending, flooding her entire being until they were both swept away by its sheer force.

When he rolled away from her, he brought her with him, cradling her gently against him, one hand pulling down the sheets that covered them to feel cool air against their heated bodies.

'What is that?' One hand touched the faint scar at her stomach.

She knew instinctively what he was referring to without even looking. 'It's my scar,' she murmured. Her eyes felt heavy, as if she were drugged with love, tiredness creeping through her sated body even though she tried hard to fight it off.

'I know it's a scar, but what from?' He gave her shoulder a little shake to try and rouse her.

'From the Caesarian. I had a difficult birth.' Her eyes

closed and she snuggled in against him. 'The whole pregnancy was difficult—I spent nearly all of it in hospital.' Her lips curved in a sleepy smile. 'That's where I was when you tried to phone me from the States. There was no other man; there never has been any other man.'

She was unaware of the rigid tension in him as he listened to her. 'There was your husband, though?' His voice sounded strange and she tried really hard to open her eyes. It was no use, she had lost her battle to the powerful forces of sleep. All she could do was shake her head before she drifted into a deep and all-consuming sleep.

She was alone in the bed when she finally woke up, the sheets and blankets firmly tucked around her. She lay for a moment looking at the empty pillow beside her, remembering the night of love, her heart twisting painfully in her breast.

Cold daylight filtered into the bedroom and with it cold reality. She had given her love unconditionally to Ryan last night, deliberately pushing the fact that he did not return her depth of feeling to the furthest recess of her mind. Emotion had intoxicated her body, making it brave. He had desired her and that had been enough—she had sufficient love inside her for both of them. She still did, she admitted calmly.

She pushed the covers back and, wrapping a sheet in a sarong-style around her body, she moved towards Sarah's room.

Her bed was empty and neatly made. Heather frowned. Judging from the neat, smooth covers, it had been attended to by an adult hand. Strange that she should have been able to sleep through it all. Sarah was not the quietest of children first thing in the morning.

Ryan must have taken her downstairs.

She moved through to the bathroom, then turned on the shower and stood under the full jet of warm water, a delicious feeling of wellbeing in her body. She hadn't realised how much she had missed the sweet tenderness of Ryan's lovemaking until last night. She wondered bleakly now how she had managed to live without it. The love she felt for him rose up inside her, so deep and intense that it hurt.

She dried her hair and dressed quickly, studying her reflection in the mirror with care. She looked radiant, her skin and eyes shone with health—or was it love? she wondered dreamily. Where would things go from here? Sudden shadows of uneasiness darkened her eyes. How would Ryan feel about her this morning? Probably no differently from the way he had yesterday, she was forced to admit. What had been love for her might just have been sex to him. That thought brought sobriety winging sharply back with a jolt, and she had to sit down for a moment at the edge of her bed.

She swallowed hard. Even if that was the case, at least she knew she had a certain power over his senses. He wanted her, even if it was only physically, and she knew now that she would accept him on those terms—she would accept him on any terms as long as he would keep her near to him.

Her heart was thudding nervously as she went downstairs. Following the sound of Sarah's noisy chatter, she went into the kitchen.

The child was sitting at the table eating some toast and she jumped up as Heather came in, running around to give her a kiss.

'Good morning, Ms Edwards.' The housekeeper smiled over at her. 'I hope you don't mind, but I took the liberty of dressing Sarah and making her some breakfast. Mr Jameson asked me not to disturb you.'

'No, of course not, that was very good of you,' Heather murmured absently, her mind very firmly on other things. 'Where is Ryan?'

'He had to go out, there was an urgent call from his office.' Mrs Marton poured her some coffee and laid a place for her at the table.

'Oh!' Heather sat down, a feeling of acute disappointment piercing her. 'I hope he will be able to get into Manchester safely with all this snow.'

'I'm sure the roads will have been cleared by now,' Mrs Marton soothed.

Heather frowned. Why hadn't Ryan woken her this morning? He could have taken Sarah and her back into Manchester with him. They could hardly stay here for much longer without any changes of clothing. 'Did Ryan leave any message for me?'

'Just that you were to wait for him and I wasn't to give you the keys for the Alfa.' The housekeeper grinned. 'No matter how desperately you pleaded.'

Heather had to laugh at that. 'What a merciless person he is,' she quipped lightly.

The day seemed to drag very slowly, probably because Heather was watching the clock all the time, waiting for Ryan's return.

She took a walk with Sarah just before lunch. It was a beautiful day—the sky was a brilliant, sharp blue and the sun was blinding on the white winter landscape. They went around by the stable to see Oliver and Sarah got a little bit upset with her when she wouldn't allow her to ride him. But even when one of the stable hands offered to saddle the pony up, Heather remained adamant. She didn't feel safe or confident letting the child ride without Ryan to supervise them. Even now the extent of her trust in Ryan amazed her. Yesterday she hadn't felt the slightest alarm at Sarah's riding, because she had known instinctively that with Ryan she would be guarded and protected. He would never take any risks with her safety.

Sarah had a sleep mid-afternoon and Heather sat in the library in front of a roaring fire, trying to concentrate on a book. She gave up after she had re-read one paragraph four times without knowing what it was about, and placed the book down on the table. So instead she stared into the flames of the fire and tried to work out what she would say to Ryan when he came back.

The sound of a car engine brought her sharply to her feet and she dashed across to the window, her heart thundering nervously.

The car that ground to a halt at the front door was not Ryan's. It was a sleek red sports car and, as Heather watched, a door opened and one trim ankle clad in a designer shoe appeared.

Her heart sank dismally as she recognised Annabel in the silver-fox coat, her blonde hair falling in a sleek, sophisticated style around her shoulders.

Heather's blood ran cold as she returned to her seat by the fire. She had wanted to forget that woman's very existence. The naïveté of such an intention was brought forcibly home to her now. Annabel was not the type of woman to stand back in the shadows, even if Ryan would want her to, which he probably did not.

The door opened and the other woman marched in. Heather didn't much care for the expression on her face. The pleasant, carefully controlled look that Annabel usually exuded around Ryan was nowhere to be seen.

'Hello, Annabel.' Heather rose politely to her feet.

'I'm afraid Ryan isn't here.'

'Yes, I know.' Annabel made no attempt at social niceties. Her eyes raked over Heather with an almost contemptuous light in them before she moved to sit down on one of the settees. She was wearing a black Dior suit, its line simple yet elegant. Her only jewellery was a diamond brooch in the shape of a true lovers' knot that sparkled on her lapel. 'I met him for lunch in Manchester.'

'Oh.' Heather sank back down into her seat, her misery at that piece of information almost overflowing.

'We had quite a talk, actually—all about you,' the woman continued in a hard, brittle tone.

'Couldn't you find anything better to talk about?' Heather's temper was starting to rise to her rescue now, at this blatantly aggressive attitude.

There was a tap at the door interrupting whatever Annabel's reply would have been and Mrs Marton came in. 'Can I get you anything, Ms Rothstar?'

Annabel flicked a glance at her diamond wristwatch. 'Yes, I'll have a black coffee. Make it quick, will you? I've only come back to pack, then I'm going straight back to Manchester.'

'Very well.' The housekeeper sent an enquiring look towards Heather and she shook her head.

'Nothing for me, thank you.' She waited until the door had closed again before turning back to Annabel. 'Do I gather from that that you are leaving?'

'Yes, you do.' Annabel crossed her long legs, showing a shapely glimpse of knee and thigh. 'We have decided that it's best if I stay at Ryan's Manchester apartment until he sorts out this thing with you.' The woman's voice was perfectly controlled, almost as if she were discussing the weather, only her eyes were wild with fury. 'You do realise that you are making a complete fool of yourself, I suppose?'

'No?' Heather's face was an impassive mask, successfully hiding the turmoil within. 'But I presume you are about to enlighten me.'

'I am talking about the way you are throwing yourself at Ryan,' Annabel replied without compunction. 'He is in love with me and you are making a very big mistake.'

There was a deathly silence for a moment. 'I think it is you who are making the mistake, Annabel, because Ryan has asked me to marry him.'

Afterwards Heather was to wonder where on earth those words had sprung from in such a calm, serene tone. She hadn't consciously been aware of the words formulating in her mind. They had had the desired effect, though. Annabel's composure was shattered for a moment, the delicate glowing skin changing to a strangely ashen colour.

'And I suppose you imagine he's asked you because he loves you,' the scornful voice lashed out after a moment. The blonde head shook in an emphatic denial of that. 'The only reason he's asking you is because you are giving something that I'm not prepared to give. A child.' The red lips curved in a triumphant smile. 'He asked you to marry him because of your child.'

The door had opened in the middle of Annabel's angry tirade, and she swung her head around now. 'I don't want any coffee——'

The words died on her lips as both women suddenly noticed that it wasn't Mrs Marton but Ryan who stood in the doorway.

'That was quite a speech,' he drawled, his body strangely still, his eyes narrowed on Annabel. 'Care to explain it?'

For once Annabel was lost for words, and she seemed to be shrinking visibly into the upholstery.

'Well? I'm waiting.' The words were somehow all the more intimidating because of the quiet way in which Ryan delivered them. His gaze moved over towards Heather, roving over her pale face in a curiously gentle way.

'Annabel has been telling me why you proposed to me,' Heather told him, a slight tremor in her soft voice.

'Really?' His glance was winging back to the other woman now, one dark eyebrow raised. 'That is remarkable, considering I have never discussed anything but business with you. Have you taken up mind-reading, by any chance?' Before the woman had a chance to say anything Ryan continued, 'Because if so I'd drop it, if I were you—you're no damn good at it. For your information, I asked Heather to marry me for the simple reason that I love her—no other reason, just that.'

Heather stared up at him, hardly daring to believe what he was saying, her heart beating so loudly that she had difficulty in hearing what he was saying now.

'And as our business arrangements are now finished I suggest you pack your bags and leave.'

Annabel rose to her feet at that. 'Don't worry, I'm going,' she told him, with a defiant toss of her blonde hair.

Heather had to admire the way she calmly crossed the room with her head held high. Only the vicious way that she slammed the door behind her spoiled the dignified effect.

The silence between Ryan and Heather seemed to stretch into infinity after she left, but in actual fact it could only have been seconds before Ryan came to kneel down at the side of her chair.

'I'm sorry, Heather,' he whispered softly.

For a moment she just looked at him, her eyes drinking in those darkly handsome features. 'Sorry for what?' Her voice was soft and husky. 'That you lied to Annabel about loving me?'

'Lied to her?' he muttered in a strangely dazed tone. 'I've never faced that truth more clearly in my life.' He looked into the wide darkness of her eyes. 'Just tell me that you don't hate me, Heather; please tell me that you don't hate me for the way I've treated you, the things I've said.'

She lifted a hand tentatively to touch the strained, worried lines of his face, shaking her head in wonderment. 'Why on earth should I hate you, Ryan?'

He caught that hand in a grip that was fierce and intense. 'When you told me this morning how you had suffered through your pregnancy alone, how you had always been alone, I hated myself for what I'd put you through, for the things that I'd said to you. I had to get up, leave the house. I felt too damned ashamed to look you in the eye.' He took a long, deep breath. 'The only thing I can say in my defence is that I've been so eaten up with jealousy that I haven't been able to see straight. When you left the apartment in London I was consumed with it. I arrived back four days after our argument on the phone, expecting to be able to iron out our problems in the one minute it took me to ask you to marry me. But you were gone and, try as I did, I couldn't trace you at all.'

'You came back to ask me . . .?' Heather's voice trailed off as tears sprung into her eyes. They could only have missed each other by a mere fraction, because that was the day she had moved out to the hotel. If she had waited just one more day . . .Tears streamed down her cheeks at the cruel irony of fate.

'Don't cry, honey.' His voice was anguished as he pulled her into his arms, cradling her body close.

'Did you really search for me?' She curled trembling arms up and around his neck.

'I must have tried every damn advertising agency in London,'he muttered grimly.

'I was in a hotel for a little while, but then they had to take me into hospital because I was in danger of losing Sarah.' She turned her head against his neck, breathing in the warm familiar aroma of his cologne. The strength of his arms helped to steady her sobs. 'I was so frightened, Ryan. I wanted you so much.'

She felt the tremor of his response shudder through his body at that. 'Heather, can you ever forgive me? If I hadn't been so caught up in business, if——'

She touched the side of his face with her lips, effectively bringing his words to a halt. 'If I had told you about the baby in the first place, then none of this would have happened,' she reminded him grimly. 'But my fear and my pride wouldn't let me. I didn't want you to stay around out of duty, I wanted your love.'

'And that was the one thing you always had,' he admitted softly. 'Even though I didn't acknowledge that fact until I came back from the States and it was too late. I thought that I was going out of my mind when I couldn't find you. I tried desperately to deny the love I felt for you, to tell myself that you were no good, heartless, scheming. Anything to get rid of the yearning empty feeling inside me. When I learned that you had married a wealthy businessman I . . .' His voice deepened with such emotion that she could hardly bear it.

'There's only ever been one man in my life, and that's you, Ryan,' she whispered through her tears. 'And it's not too late, not when we've been given a second chance and I love you so very much.'

It was much later before they were able to talk again. Ryan had picked her up in strong arms, carrying her upstairs to his room, a look on his face that had melted every bone in her body.

'Now tell me that again,' he had demanded in a voice slurred with passion as he placed her down on the silk covers of his bed. And she did, again and again.

It was as he turned her in his arms that her eyes fell on the silver photograph frame beside them. Her breath caught in her throat and her lips parted in a gasp.

He moved to see what she was looking at and smiled. 'Beautiful, isn't she?' He bent his head to place a kiss on the vulnerable curve of her neck, almost as if he were tasting her. 'But I much prefer her in the flesh,' he growled huskily.

She looked up at him tremulously, her face glowing with happiness. 'I thought when I first saw it that it was a picture of Annabel,' she told him. 'I'd forgotten that snap of me.'

He sat up slightly to look down at her. 'There has never been anything between me and Annabel.' His face was grave, his voice serious. 'The only thing we have ever had in common was business, Heather. Up until this morning she still owned five per cent of my company—a fact that I have now had remedied after a long struggle. I know she had a stupid crush on me once, but I thought that was all over. Simon assured me before I invited them here that he had asked her to marry him, and it was a foregone conclusion that she would accept.'

Heather frowned. How could she have been so stupid,

so blind? 'So you have never asked her to marry you?'

'What? Are you crazy?' He pulled her roughly into his arms again. 'That is a question I will only ever ask one woman, with no regrets,' he told her forcibly.

"INDULGE A LITTLE" SWEEPSTAKES

HERE'S HOW THE SWEEPSTAKES WORKS

NO PURCHASE NECESSARY

To enter each drawing, complete the appropriate Official Entry Form or a 3" by 5" index card by hand-printing your name, address and phone number and the trip destination that the entry is being submitted for (i.e., Walt Disney World Vacation Drawing, etc.) and mailing it to: Indulge '91 Subscribers-Only Sweepstakes, P.O. Box 1397, Buffalo, New York 14269-1397.

No responsibility is assumed for lost, late or misdirected mail. Entries must be sent separately with first class postage affixed, and be received by: 9/30/91 for the Walt Disney World Vacation Drawing, 10/31/91 for the Alaskan Cruise Drawing and 11/30/91 for the Hawaiian Vacation Drawing. Sweepstakes is open to residents of the U.S. and Canada, 21 years of age or older as of 11/7/91.

For complete rules, send a self-addressed, stamped (WA residents need not affix return postage) envelope to: Indulge '91 Subscribers-Only Sweepstakes Rules, P.O. Box 4005, Blair, NE 68009.

© 1991 HARLEQUIN ENTERPRISES LTD.   DIR-RL

"INDULGE A LITTLE" SWEEPSTAKES

HERE'S HOW THE SWEEPSTAKES WORKS

NO PURCHASE NECESSARY

To enter each drawing, complete the appropriate Official Entry Form or a 3" by 5" index card by hand-printing your name, address and phone number and the trip destination that the entry is being submitted for (i.e., Walt Disney World Vacation Drawing, etc.) and mailing it to: Indulge '91 Subscribers-Only Sweepstakes, P.O. Box 1397, Buffalo, New York 14269-1397.

No responsibility is assumed for lost, late or misdirected mail. Entries must be sent separately with first class postage affixed, and be received by: 9/30/91 for the Walt Disney World Vacation Drawing, 10/31/91 for the Alaskan Cruise Drawing and 11/30/91 for the Hawaiian Vacation Drawing. Sweepstakes is open to residents of the U.S. and Canada, 21 years of age or older as of 11/7/91.

For complete rules, send a self-addressed, stamped (WA residents need not affix return postage) envelope to: Indulge '91 Subscribers-Only Sweepstakes Rules, P.O. Box 4005, Blair, NE 68009.

© 1991 HARLEQUIN ENTERPRISES LTD.   DIR-RL

INDULGE A LITTLE—WIN A LOT!

Summer of '91 Subscribers-Only Sweepstakes

OFFICIAL ENTRY FORM

This entry must be received by: Sept. 30, 1991
This month's winner will be notified by: Oct. 7, 1991
Trip must be taken between: Nov. 7, 1991—Nov. 7, 1992

YES, I want to win the Walt Disney World® vacation for two. I understand the prize includes round-trip airfare, first-class hotel and pocket money as revealed on the "wallet" scratch-off card.

Name _____

Address _____ Apt. _____

City _____

State/Prov. _____ Zip/Postal Code _____

Daytime phone number _____
(Area Code)

Return entries with invoice in envelope provided. Each book in this shipment has two entry coupons—and the more coupons you enter, the better your chances of winning!

© 1991 HARLEQUIN ENTERPRISES LTD.   CPS-M1